EVERYBODY MAKES MISTAKES

A mutilated body is found on a lonely street in Reykjavík. Detective Grímur intends to see that justice is done. Kjartan Jónsson vows that his daughter's killer will be punished. And that the punishment will fit the crime. Prime suspect Gunnar Atli desperately needs to prevent his own dark secrets from coming to light. And he's not the only one.

Fine lines separate truth, justice and vengeance. Put a foot wrong, and any one of them could be making the biggest mistake of his life.

In Iceland, the winter shadows grow long...

#3

THE MISTAKE

GRANT NICOL

#13 Press
ntp-13a03

#

PUBLISHED BY NUMBER THIRTEEN PRESS

PRINT VERSION 1.0

#

#1

A SMALL PAIR of blood-splattered feet were the first things Snorri Pétursson saw as he swung the beam of his flickering torch across the snow-covered lava field. They looked so foreign in such a place that at first he thought he had to be seeing things. When he ran the light further up the legs across the torn black tights and black skirt he could see that the young woman they belonged to was no longer alive. Her eyes were wide open but staring lifelessly ahead at nothing, covered with a thin layer of blood that criss-crossed her cornea like a fishing net. Her startled appearance gave her a look of being taken completely by surprise. By the state of her head that was exactly what had happened. The damage her small frame had suffered had been truly devastating. It would have been difficult to do more damage to her with a baseball bat.

Snorri shuddered as he thought of what she had gone through. He tried to rub some warmth into his arms through his jacket as the cold started to take root in his limbs. He wasn't sure if it was the face of the dead girl or the increasingly heavy snow that was gathering on his shoulders that was responsible but he had started to shiver. The dark around him was impenetrable. Beyond the tiny radius of his torch was a void so complete he could have been on another planet. What a strange place to die he thought. So cold, so alone and so very far from home. Wherever home was. What could have possibly led her to this place?

He turned his attention to the upside-down car nearby and tried to picture the order in which events had played out. When the car had rolled she must have flown head-first through the windscreen straight into the treacherously uneven rocks. There was no way she could have possibly been wearing a seatbelt. A big mistake. It would be hard to say which impact had done the most damage but the end result had certainly never been in doubt.

The top right-hand corner of her skull had been torn away leaving a flap of flesh and bone hanging by a thread or two of bloody tissue. An eerie window into the recess of her cranial cavity. It was a part of her that no one should have ever seen. At least the end would have come quickly.

Her shock, great as it might have been, would have been mercifully short-lived. He stumbled over to the wreck and inspected the interior for signs of life. As he took his hat off and scratched his bald head something struck him as not quite right. A pair of shoes with their shoelaces tied together, inside the car, lying on the upturned ceiling.

It was as if they had been sitting on or near one of the front seats when the car had turned over. That in itself wasn't too unusual, the dead girl was after all barefoot and her shoes must have gone somewhere. But these were big, way too big for a girl of her stature. They were men's basketball boots, at least size 11. Many sizes too big for her little feet. The owner of the shoes had to be at least 6 feet tall and she would have struggled to make 5' 6" in a pair of high-heels. Maybe she hadn't been alone in the car; that was the only explanation he could think of. He ran his torch beam across the back seat looking for clues as to who might have been with her. Amongst the mess of shopping bags and food wrappers he saw an empty bottle of Brennivín. That would go a long way to explaining how the car had crashed. It was possible she hadn't even been driving at the time of the accident. Maybe someone else had been, the Brennivín drinker perhaps, and that was what had caused the car to roll over onto its roof.

He was going to have to make a more thorough search of the area now just in case there was someone else who needed help, or had to be arrested, or both. If there had been another occupant it would have been reasonable to expect them to stay as close to the car as possible. Unless of course, they had something to hide.

The snow was whipping around him now as the wind

picked up and turned the strengthening downfall into a whirling dervish's dance around his face. The going would be slow and tedious, every step he took he would have to check where he was putting his feet so they didn't go down a crack or a hole that would turn his night into an absolute disaster. A sprained ankle all the way out here in the middle of nowhere was the last thing he needed. The circumstances called for a slow and methodical approach. He would need to stay calm and remind himself that while the girl was beyond help there still might be someone else out there who needed his assistance.

Luckily for Snorri he didn't have too long to wait for the answer to his dilemma. Not more than twenty feet from the girl's body another figure lay motionless in the snow. His initial reaction was that he had another fatality on his hands. He knelt down next to the man who had also lost his shoes during his ill-fated evening and reached to feel for a pulse in his neck. There were no obvious wounds on him as there were on the girl. Despite the lack of any signs of life he appeared to have come through the crash in relatively good shape. For a dead man. His face was lifeless and his eyes closed but there was very little blood on him. He looked almost peaceful, as if death had brought with it a great relief of sorts.

Yet as soon as Snorri's fingers touched his neck, the dead man opened his eyes and began to scream. Although Snorri had barely made contact the man's torment was undeniable. Snorri pulled his fingers away as fast as he could, hoping to put an end to the hideous noise emanating from the poor soul but it made no difference whatsoever. He put his hands over his ears and backed

4

away. From a safer distance he stared helplessly at the tortured creature and wondered what the hell he had stumbled across in the middle of the Icelandic night.

\#

NINE YEARS LATER

\#

#2

STARING BACK AT him was a man he no longer recognised nor wanted to know. Gunnar Atli Davíðsson hated the face in the mirror and today he felt even worse than he looked. A headache the size of the Faxaflói Bay had a grip on him and didn't feel as if it would be letting go any time soon. Dizzy spells had plagued him for the last week. One had actually caused him to faint while standing over the sink at work. The unmistakeable signs of a man falling apart. The skin down the side of his arms started to tingle so he took a deep draught of cold water from the tap and hoped it would pass. When he closed his eyes the light above the bathroom mirror pulsed through his eyelids as if it were alive. Then everything slowly turned as black as the middle of a moonless night.

When he came to, the right side of his face felt as cold as ice. Snow was landing on him softly like feathers from a ruptured pillow. At first he thought he might have suffered a stroke and was half-expecting to be paralysed down one side of his body. One by one he tested his limbs to see if they still worked. They all did. He eased his eyes open and was relieved to find he wasn't lying in the middle of the street. It was in fact the tiny paved garden in front of his apartment block. Apparently after making it down the stairs from his flat on the first floor he had passed out in the snow, practically at his front door. He tried to push himself upright but decided it was an unnecessarily risky move. If history had taught him one thing it was that it was prudent in these situations to take your time getting up unless you wanted to wind up back on your arse straight away. Though it was dark out and the street lights were partially obscured by the old leafless tree and scraggly ferns that sat along the fence, his surroundings began to come into focus.

He could see footprints in the fine coating of snow that had fallen overnight but it was hard to know whether they belonged to him or not. He thought it unlikely that they were all his. There just seemed to be too many of them. When he straightened his back he could see across to the rubbish bins in the corner by the fence. The black one was where it always sat but the blue one for recycling was sitting at an odd angle as though someone had leant against it or pushed it out of the way. It was hard to see exactly what it was but there was definitely something hidden behind it as though one of his neighbours had tried to stash a bundle of rubbish where they obviously were not supposed to. The harder he tried to focus on whatever it was lying behind the bin the more blurred everything became so he closed his eyes for a minute and tried to relax. When he opened them again he could see what it was, even if he wished almost straight away that he'd kept his eyes shut.

It was a pair of legs, there was no doubt about that. They looked a little like the ones used in shop windows but it wasn't a mannequin. They were the real thing and every inch of them was covered in cuts or bruises. Some of them tiny, some of them huge. Things were even worse than he had feared. He tried once again to get his face off the paving stone and this time was able to do so without feeling as though he was going to pass out. He dragged himself partially upright and leant back against the front of the building so he was sitting facing the bins and their ghastly companion. A little vomit dribbled onto his shirt front. He shoved a handful of snow into his mouth to get rid of the taste of bile. He could see more of the legs now and who they were attached to as well. The girl lay naked and lifeless. Whatever had happened to her had been extraordinarily violent. She was covered in contusions and abrasions from the top of her head to the tips of her toes. The worst of them were on her face. She had been cut from both corners of her mouth all the way up her cheeks in a ghastly facsimile of a smile like some horrid sideshow clown.

He fought off the urge to vomit again and wiped the sweat from his forehead, even though the mercury was well below zero. How long since his last clear memory? He tried frantically to clear his head. According to his phone it had been fifteen minutes since he last looked at it and that had been as he hurried to the bathroom. How on earth could it take quarter of an hour to brush your teeth and get down a flight of stairs? He couldn't remember walking a single step of the journey but when he turned towards the front door he could see that he'd even left it slightly ajar as he left the building.

With an effort he crawled towards her feet and touched one of them. It was cold and waxy and no longer felt human in the slightest. The cuts on her were fresh and varied. She had been subjected to the most thorough of mutilations. No space on her body had been left untouched. Nothing had been spared, tattooed in the ink of hate by someone displaying incredible patience. Enough to match their dedication to cruelty.

He felt the nausea rise within him again and this time it easily won the battle for control. He turned his head just in time and vomited. The warmth of his stomach's watery contents melted a hole in the snow and slowly disappeared into the gaps between the paving stones. He forced himself to his feet and leant against the building for a minute. A bad feeling worked all the way through his body. It wouldn't do for him to be found in such a compromising situation. He wasn't sure if he should call for help or just run away while he still had the chance.

Flashing lights from the street suddenly bathed the old tree and the surrounding walls in crazy carousel-like colours. The garden took on the atmosphere of a carnival of the damned, ugly and garish. A police car pulled up just outside the apartments and two uniformed figures of the Reykjavík police force leapt from the vehicle. They were on him before he knew what was happening.

His ability to react quickly had been left upstairs with the rest of his mental faculties. Strong hands grabbed his arms and pulled them behind his back before handcuffing his wrists in place. He was pinned against the building by the taller of the two officers who obviously couldn't tell that he was barely able to stand without assistance.

'You don't understand,' he whimpered.

'Well then you had better explain it to us,' the tall one said.

'Jesus, look at this,' said the other.

He knelt down next to the dead girl, getting as close to her as he could stomach. He rubbed his hand over his face and let out a low whistle.

'Keep a good grip on him, Helgi. You've never seen anything like this in your life.'

'Don't worry, he won't be getting away,' Helgi replied.

'Let's get him in the car and get some help.'

'You don't understand,' Gunnar Atli repeated.

'You don't say. Exactly what is it I don't understand? Maybe you'd better start from the very beginning and enlighten us. And you can take a seat in our car while you're doing it. How does that sound?'

Helgi grabbed Gunnar Atli roughly by the shoulder and spun him around so the two of them were facing each other.

'I'm not responsible for any of this. I'm very sorry it's

happened, but it's not my fault.'

'Why is that exactly? I don't see anyone else whose fault this might have been. So why don't you tell me, what is it I'm missing here?'

'I'm not at all well,' Gunnar Atli whispered. 'I have this condition.'

'He has a condition,' Helgi mimicked.

'She has a condition too. Commonly known as dead.'

Gunnar Atli was pallid and sweaty despite the freezing temperature of the early morning. The shorter officer took a few steps closer to the two of them to get a better look as well.

'He's right you know. He doesn't look right at all.'

'Neither would you if you'd just done that to someone,' snarled Helgi.

'You got a point there. What did she do to you? To make you do that to her? She must have really pissed you off. Let's get him in the car.'

Helgi pulled him away from the building and towards the parked car. He opened the back door and pushed Gunnar Atli down into the seat before climbing into the front. He picked up the radio and called headquarters.

'The caller was right. There's a body here and we've arrested a suspect at the scene. You'd better send someone to collect her. She's beyond any sort of medical aid, God help her.'

'I told you, I didn't do that,' Gunnar Atli complained from the back seat.

Helgi turned around to stare down Gunnar Atli.

'Did you hear that, Gulli?' he shouted through the door. 'He says he didn't do it. Should we just let him go then?'

Helgi laughed as if it was the funniest thing he'd ever heard.

When Gunnar Atli hung his head in surrender Helgi turned his attention back to the radio.

'The suspect claims to have a medical condition. You'd better send an ambulance just in case.'

Gulli got into the passenger seat with a morbid expression on his face. He wiped the perspiration from his brow.

'I've seen some pretty awful stuff in my time,' he said. 'But that really makes me feel sick. I've always felt that it's important to give people the benefit of the doubt but you might just be the one who ends all that.'

Helgi put the radio down and turned to his companion.

'What do you mean?'

'What hope is there for anyone who'd do that to another person? That's what I mean.'

The two of them stared at Gunnar Atli waiting for an answer. He in turn stared at his lap unwilling to meet their gaze. Helgi reached over and shook Gunnar Atli by the shoulder.

'He's talking to you. What the hell is wrong with you? That's what we want to know.'

Gunnar Atli shook his head slowly as if trying to find a rhythm that would keep him calm. Behind the three of them at the top of the street a black Mercedes had been sitting in the shadows, its driver carefully hidden from view. While the two police officers looked at Gunnar Atli and waited for help to arrive the car pulled out of its parking space and slowly drove off down Barónsstígur towards the city centre. When it was safely out of sight it turned its headlights on and disappeared into the night.

#3

DETECTIVE GRÍMUR KARLSSON was waiting for him at the front door of the city morgue. They shook hands and introduced themselves. Grímur said something about how sorry he was. Kjartan nodded and suggested they get in out of the cold. They walked downstairs together in silence. There was nothing to say that wouldn't sound trite. It was no time for small talk. Grímur put his hand on the door of the room where the body was being kept but didn't open it. The two men looked at each other, both unsure.

'As I said to you earlier on the phone, she has sustained

many injuries. You are going to find this rather upsetting. More upsetting than you might have imagined, I'm afraid.'

Kjartan nodded but couldn't make eye contact with Grímur yet. He was pleased he hadn't allowed Helga to accompany him, he had been right to trust his instincts and put his foot down. There was no way she would have been able to deal with this without going off the deep end. He took a deep breath filled with resignation and defeat and signalled that he was ready. Grímur pushed the door open.

Inside was a large cool room with a single stainless steel table in the centre. The table held a body covered with a stiff, clean white sheet. The reality of the job Kjartan had been summoned to do finally hit home. He wanted to run to his daughter and take her in his arms even though he knew that to do so would be bordering on the insane. There had never been anything he hadn't been able to protect her from, except herself maybe. Her worst enemy had been her need to do everything on her own. Grímur slowly lifted the sheet to reveal the ghastly face beneath. Her grotesque smile, if that's what it was, would stay with her forever more, now that there was no longer anything left for them to smile about.

Kjartan reached down and touched the ruptured flesh of her cheek. He flinched when he felt the wound and hated himself for doing it. Even though she barely looked like his daughter anymore he still felt it was wrong to pull away like that.

'What kind of sick bastard did this to you?'

He looked up at the detective, but Grímur didn't have an answer either.

'What did you do to your hair?' Kjartan asked as if she were still capable of answering. 'You used to have such pretty long hair.'

Her hair was very short and very blonde. There was a tiny amount of dark regrowth showing underneath so the dye-job was recent, a week old maybe but not much longer.

'Why would she do that?' he asked no one in particular. As he ran his fingers through her bleach-blonde hair a tear ran down his cheek and dropped onto the sheet. He tried to brush it away as if he had somehow soiled a pristine landscape.

'There are many questions we are going to have to answer before we can understand what happened to her. We need to recreate the last months of her life. Then we may be able to get to the bottom of this,' Grímur said.

Kjartan moved to pull the sheet off the rest of her body but Grímur placed his hand on it and wouldn't let him.

'That's not necessary. All we require is a yes or a no. Is this your daughter?'

'Of course this is my daughter. Do you think I'd still be standing here if it wasn't? I want to see what else he did to her. Don't think for a minute that you get to choose what I see today and what I don't. You wake me up at six-thirty to tell me that you think my daughter's dead. Don't you dare tell me what to do! You will let me pull this sheet back and look at her or I will hit you so hard you won't know what day it is.'

Grímur thought about standing his ground but then tried putting himself in Kjartan's shoes for a moment. He dragged the sheet away to let him see the full extent of her injuries. She was covered with mutilations of every size

19

and shape. There were small incisions that had been made at an angle to leave flaps of dangling skin. Some looked as though the exposed flesh had then been burned with a cigarette lighter or a match. Some were tiny and round and deep as if a screwdriver had been used. The cuts on her face went all the way through to her teeth. Even her gums had been cut in the killer's fury. Whoever had done this to her hadn't wanted to merely end her life, they had wanted her to leave the world kicking and screaming. Grímur pointed to one incision slightly larger than the others but otherwise indistinguishable from the rest. It lay near the top left-hand corner of her left breast.

'An initial examination suggests that this may have been the wound that killed her but we won't know for certain until after a full autopsy.'

He replaced the sheet over her face and tidied up the corners so she looked nice and neat again. Kjartan composed himself and then looked Grímur right in the eye.

'Can we go now?'

Grímur nodded and led them out of the room. As they walked back upstairs a forensic technician in a white lab coat walked past them. Kjartan stared and wondered if that was the man who would be cutting his little girl open in a few minutes. The look he got back suggested that he would be.

Fifteen minutes later they were in Grímur's office at police headquarters on Hverfisgata sitting on opposite sides of his desk. Kjartan had kept silent during the drive from the morgue and Grímur had allowed him the time to absorb the shock of what he'd just seen. He now wrapped his hands around a cup of coffee Grímur had fetched for him and stared intently at it. The last thing in the world that he felt like doing now was talking.

'I'm going to have to ask you some questions about Ísabella. We could put it off for a few hours but the sooner we get it done the better.'

'Bella, everyone just called her Bella.'

'Okay, Bella it is. We need to put together a picture of the last few months of her life. Where she went, who she knew, that sort of thing. If we can talk to the people she was spending time with then we'll have a much better idea of what might have happened. Can we start with the last time you saw her?'

Kjartan looked up at Grímur briefly but had to look away again to hide the embarrassment in his eyes.

'We hadn't seen her in six months. It makes me feel responsible for what happened to her, not insisting that she come home where she would be safe. She could be so stubborn, so much like me. When she got an idea in her head it was impossible to get it out again.'

He tried his coffee and set it down on the table again before continuing.

'She had a fight with someone at her sister's wedding, or at least that's what we think happened. I guess we'll never know one way or the other now.'

'What happened after the fight?'

'She disappeared. No note, not a word to anyone. We didn't even get a phone call for a month and then she wouldn't tell us why she'd run away or where she was. We always assumed it was Reykjavík but we never knew for sure until today. Her mother's been beside herself waiting for... dreading that this day would come.'

Kjartan rested his head in his hands and took a moment to compose himself.

'When was the last time you heard from her?'

'Her sister talked to her about a week ago. They argued and blamed each other for what happened. I think Bella was angry at all the attention that was lavished on Abelína at her wedding but what are you supposed to do when one of your children finally gets married? If we'd waited for someone to ask Bella...'

Kjartan struggled to get the words out as they stuck in his throat

'Take your time.'

Kjartan stared at his cup of coffee as if it could somehow answer the questions for him. He was holding it so tight that his knuckles had gone white.

'Then of course Abelína got mad after the wedding because all the attention was suddenly on Bella and her disappearing act. That was probably her plan all along. Her way of turning the tables on her sister. She was pretty talented at that. Never one to be bested in a fight, again just like her dad.

'Bella accused her sister of being selfish and not being able to see anything from anyone else's point of view. Which was true I guess. But Abelína had seen her big day overshadowed by her sister running off and was upset. They said a few things that they shouldn't have and that was the last we ever heard from her.

'As you can imagine, Abelína's a mess. The last thing she told Bella was that she wished she was dead. You've no idea when you're saying things like that that they might be the very last words you say to someone.'

Grímur leaned back in his chair and wondered how he'd feel if it were him on the other side of the desk. He didn't want to push Kjartan for answers but they had to put together a picture of what she had been doing if they were going to solve her murder.

'So you have no idea who she might have been socialising with here or where she might have been spending her time?'

'None whatsoever. She became something of a mystery. I got the feeling the only reason she rang from time to time was to let us know she was still alive and that there was no point in looking for her. I guess I just hoped she would come to her senses sooner or later and come home. Like when an angry child runs off and finally has to head back to the only place it knows when it gets hungry and tired. Only she never got lonely or hungry. Well, she never came home anyway.'

'Let's take a moment to gather our thoughts. I think we could both do with a break.'

'No, it's okay. I want to get this out of the way. Ask your questions and let's get this over with. I don't want to have to go through this twice.'

'I understand. Did she ever mention any friends, a boyfriend perhaps?'

'No, nothing like that. We were completely in the dark as to what she might have been getting up to here. That's why it hasn't come as that much of a surprise. I had a feeling that she would get herself into trouble. You have these feelings about your children, don't you?'

Grímur furrowed his brow a little as he took a moment to answer.

'I suppose you do.'

'You don't have any children of your own?'

'No.'

'The only thing they're guaranteed to do is break your heart. Do you have any suspects yet?'

'There was a man found at the scene.'

'So you've got the guy already?'

'We've arrested him and he's in custody at the moment but we're still waiting to interview him.'

'What the hell are you waiting for?'

'He will be questioned shortly when a lawyer is available. I don't want you to get your hopes up though, it's not as open and shut a case as we might have hoped for.'

'What exactly do you mean by that?'

'Although he was found at the scene with your daughter's body there is no physical evidence linking him to her death. We've searched his flat and nothing inside indicates she was killed there. He says he was on his way to work when he came across her and that part seems to check out but the rest of his story is odd to say the least.'

'What do you mean by odd?'

'Apparently he has these episodes where he blacks out briefly and then comes around again a few minutes later feeling disorientated and confused. He told us that there's fifteen minutes he can't account for just before we found him with her.'

'You're kidding me, you're actually going to believe that crap?'

'Right now I don't know what to believe. I'm taking it one step at a time so we don't get ahead of ourselves. I suggest you do the same. He says he didn't know your daughter, but that part was less convincing.'

'But you're happy to believe the rest of the rubbish he's told you?'

'Like I said, there's plenty we need to explore.'

'Don't give me that wishy-washy shit.'

Kjartan was leaning across the table now as if by doing so he could will the answer he wanted out of Grímur. Grímur held his hands up as if to signal that enough was enough.

'We'll need to have a much clearer picture of what happened before the prosecutor will consider charging anyone. We will hold him until such time as that decision has been made. I assume you will be heading back to Leirubakki now. We may well need to get in touch with you again shortly. It would be good for us to know where you are.'

Kjartan took his seat again rather reluctantly and stared across the table. The colour had returned to his cheeks with a vengeance, he was flushed with anger.

'No, I'm going to be staying here in Reykjavík for a while. There's some things I need to attend to. Can I see where she was living?'

'Not at the moment, for now it's got to be considered a crime scene but we'll let you know when we can release her belongings to you.'

'My family are going to need to know what happened to her and as soon as possible. We haven't seen her for six months and now...'

He threw his arms up in the air in exasperation before slamming them down on the table.

'This is one puzzle that absolutely cannot go unsolved. I

need answers to take back with me.'

'I understand that and you'll get them, but we need time. I can phone you and your family as soon as we know anything. There's no reason for you to stay here.'

'I'm not going anywhere until I know what happened to her.'

'I think your family would probably like to see you again, Kjartan.'

'My family will be expecting answers and that's just what they're going to get. You say you understand that. Well, do you? Do you really know what that means? They'll be expecting me to come home with our baby girl so we can bury her in the family plot and they'll be wanting to know why she's dead, who killed her and what's going to happen to him. I can't see how it could take you too long to find out those things for us even if you do need to wait for his lawyer to get out of bed this morning. No one came to hold my hand today. No one came to tell me everything was going to be all right. And do you know why that is? It's because everything is not all right. It is not going to be all right. In fact it will never be all right ever again. What has happened to us cannot be undone.

'I'll be going home with my daughter in a coffin in a couple of days and you'd better have those answers for me by then. You have the guy you need in custody so do your job before I do it for you.'

Kjartan threw his coffee cup across the room and watched it disintegrate against the wall behind Grímur before marching out of the room.

#4

Grímur was distracted as he entered the interview room and took a seat opposite Gunnar Atli. He put two coffees down on the table and tried to remember which one was supposed to be his.

'Is one of those for me?' Gunnar Atli asked.

Grímur nodded as he realised he should have just put sugar in both of them. He eventually gave up trying to remember which was which and slid one of the cups slowly across the table.

'Here you go, we're having a short delay with your

lawyer but she'll be here soon. I thought we could start without her though, just have a chat until she gets here. That's okay, isn't it?'

'I don't know if that's such a great idea,' Gunnar Atli said and took a sip of his coffee. He grimaced slightly and put the cup down again. 'I do want to start off by telling you that I didn't kill that girl. I want to be very clear about that.'

'You've already told the officers who arrested you that you don't remember coming down the stairs of your building, how you got to be standing over her body, or for that matter any of the fifteen minutes leading up to your arrest. If that is the case then how do you expect me to believe that in spite of you having no recollection of events for a full quarter of an hour, that you're certain you had absolutely nothing to do with her death?'

'I just know.'

'You just know? But if I am to believe what you're telling me then, even if you did kill her, you probably wouldn't remember anyway, right?'

Grímur tried his own coffee and silently cursed the lack of sugar. He wished his memory was a little more reliable than it was. It was just the little things that annoyed him, like putting the ice cream away in the fridge last night instead of the freezer. They weren't the end of the world but they reminded him he was no longer a young man and that was probably the one thing he no longer needed to be reminded of. He contemplated suggesting they swap coffees but that would involve admitting he'd made a mistake and no matter how trivial it was he wasn't about to do that with a murder suspect.

'Wrong, look at my hands,' Gunnar Atli said. He held both hands up so Grímur could get a good look at them. 'Don't you think that if I'd killed her I'd have blood all over them?'

Grímur had to admit the lack of forensic evidence linking Gunnar Atli to the crime was a concern. As they spoke, Björn Magnússon was going through Gunnar Atli's first floor flat with instructions to call the moment he found anything that might suggest she had been killed there. When he'd first heard from the arresting officers about what they found he'd hoped they might have this one in the bag before the evening news. Those hopes were fading, and fading fast.

'How do I know you didn't clean yourself up? Maybe you washed your hands and don't remember that either?'

Gunnar Atli was about to reply with a sarcastic remark of his own when he reminded himself that he might come to regret it later and kept his mouth shut. He picked his coffee up again and took another sip. He might not have said anything but it was clear what he was thinking from the contemptuous grin on his face. This guy was no idiot, Grímur could see that. That was what made him so sure they had the right man. Unfortunately the onus was firmly on the police to prove that their case was anything more than circumstantial. At the moment it wasn't and both he and Gunnar Atli were aware of that.

Nína Andrésdóttir entered the room and took a seat next to her client without uttering so much as a word. She didn't acknowledge either of the men until she'd opened her briefcase and pulled out everything she might need and even then it was nothing more than a business-like smile as she straightened her jacket and put a stray hair back in its place.

'Hello, Grímur. Do you think it might be possible to have a minute or two alone with my client?'

'Sure, take your time,' Grímur said.

He had to go find some sugar for his coffee anyway so he excused himself and left them to it. He'd only just found the bag of sugar in the lunch room when his phone rang. It was Björn calling from Gunnar Atli's flat on Leifsgata.

'What's the news?'

Björn cleared his throat before answering.

'The news is, unfortunately, that there is no real news to speak of,' he said. 'If she was killed here he's managed to remove any trace of the deed whatsoever and in my opinion that's just not possible. Either you've got the wrong guy or she was killed somewhere else and then dumped outside the flats. It looks like we're back to square one. Maybe he did just come across her on his way out the door like he said.'

'But why make up all this rubbish about not remembering coming down the stairs? Does he seriously expect us to believe that there's fifteen minutes he just can't account for, and on the one day he happens to come across a dead girl on the way to work? Give me a break.'

'Maybe he does have some kind of condition that gives him blind spots.'

'Blind spots? What the hell are you talking about?'

'You know, like the places you can't quite see in your wing mirrors. You know they're there but you've got no actual proof that they're empty so you've just got to put your faith in the fact that they are.'

'That's great, Björn. Any other news for me?'

'The lady who gave us the initial identification of the victim had a spare key for the victim's flat so we've been able to get in there to have a look around too.'

'And?'

'Nothing. The place was clean, like spotless.'

'Who had the key?'

'The upstairs neighbour, Adolfína Hallsdóttir. A retired psychiatric nurse.'

'Okay. Let her know I'll be wanting to speak to her later. I'm going to be here for a while but it seems as if we may have hit a dead end for the time being.'

'Nothing is ever as simple as we'd like it to be, is it?'

'Tell me about it.'

Grímur sighed as he stirred two full teaspoons of sugar into his coffee. He ambled back to the interview room where Nína was busy making notes on one of her many pads. Gunnar Atli looked less stressed than he had a few minutes earlier which probably had something to do with having a lawyer who could do his talking for him now. Maybe Kjartan had been right. Maybe it wasn't as fair as it could be. Nína finished her note-making and turned to Grímur.

'My client has a few things he would like me to communicate to you.'

'Okay.'

'Firstly, he has a serious psychological condition which is why he can't remember what happened just before he was arrested. He has prescribed medication for his condition but stopped taking it recently possibly causing the black-outs to return. We need to get him his pills as soon as possible so he can start taking them again. And secondly, he would like to reiterate that he had nothing to do with the girl's death. The two of them were nothing more than the most casual of acquaintances, they lived on the same street, end of story. He says this is all a misunderstanding and that someone else is responsible for her death.'

Nína looked up from her pad to indicate she was done. Grímur looked at Gunnar Atli who was now studying the table surface in front of him.

'Okay, I'll arrange for someone to get your medication for you. Where is it?'

'It's on the shelf below my bathroom mirror. There's three containers, I'll need them all.'

'And then you'll remember what you've forgotten?'

'It doesn't quite work that way. It's going to take a few days for the levels of the drugs to build up in my system again. Until then I don't think I should be answering any more of your questions, and chances are I won't regain any lost memories.'

'We have a girl in the city morgue, do you understand that? I need answers and pills or no pills you're going to give them to me.'

Grímur picked up his phone and told Björn what he needed brought down to the station. Once he was done with the call he folded his arms and stared across the table at his suspect.

'How well did you know this girl, Bella?'

'She lived just up the road from me.'

'We know that already. That's not what I asked.'

'Just to say hello to. I'd see her on the street

sometimes.'

'Nothing more than that? You never went out for coffee together, the movies, spent the night together, that sort of thing?'

'That sort of thing? No, nothing like that. How long will it take for my pills to get here?'

'They'll be here soon. If they're so important, why did you stop taking them?'

'It was a kind of experiment.'

'Is that a good idea? Doctors don't normally prescribe those drugs so their patients can decide for themselves whether to take them or not. You're not a doctor are you?'

'You have no idea what they're like, they cloud everything to the point where you don't even know yourself any more. It's like walking through a fog where you can't feel happy and you can't feel sad; it's like being trapped in a cold, grey soup.'

'Have you ever been in trouble with the police before?'

'I was in a car accident years ago if you call that trouble.'

'I noticed you walking with a little difficulty before, when we brought you into the station. Is that how you got your limp?'

'Uh huh.'

'Tell me about it.'

'Why? What's it got to do with anything now?'

'I'm a curious guy and I'd like you to answer my questions, that's what it's got to do with anything now.'

'It was just before Christmas nine years ago. We were heading out of town on holiday.'

'We? Who's 'we'?'

'Me and my girlfriend, Nanna.'

'Okay, and then what happened?'

'I lost control of the car and rolled it.'

'Were you badly hurt? You must have been to get a limp like that.'

'I broke my leg in five places, that's how I got the limp.'

'How about Nanna? Was she hurt?'

'She was killed. She went through the windscreen and didn't survive the impact. Is that what you want to know? I still don't see what this has to do with Bella.'

'Probably nothing but like I said I'm a curious guy, some people think that's why I became a detective. I saw a photograph in a frame in your flat today when the forensic guys went in for a look. Was that a photograph of Nanna?'

'Yeah, that's Nanna.'

'You know who she reminded me of?'

'Not really.'

'Bella. She looked a lot like Bella, don't you think? I mean, if you ignored the fact that she'd dyed her hair recently, they'd look almost exactly the same.'

'I don't know, would they?'

'After your crash, you spent some time in Kleppspítali?'

'Yeah. Almost eight years.'

'Seven years and ten months. That's pretty much all of your twenties gone, just like that. You must have been pretty angry about something for it to take that long to get it all out of your system. Is that why you cut her face up like that?'

Gunnar Atli was about to respond when Nína cut him off with a swift movement of her hand.

'Now I don't see what this is all about. Are you going

somewhere with this, Grímur? Or do you not remember my client stating that he had nothing to do with the girl's death? You appear to have the two incidents confused. I'm sure a car accident all those years ago has nothing at all to do with what we're here to discuss today.'

'I was just thinking out loud, that's all. Seven years and ten months is a long time to spend in a psychiatric hospital. I bet you there's a story there somewhere.'

#5

THE FIRST THING Kjartan had to do once he was out of the morgue was call Helga and tell her that he'd seen Bella, it was definitely her and their little girl was dead. Helga had taken it badly even though any other outcome would have been unlikely at best.

Today would now and for evermore be remembered as the day their world fell apart.

He hung up feeling doubly exhausted after his early start but there was work to do and he meant to do it. His first port of call was going to be Aron Steinn and Áskell. He had no idea where to find them but knew Aron Steinn's parents well enough. He called, told them the terrible news and then asked if he could have an address for their son and the shiftless lay-abouts he called his friends. At first they had been suspicious but after he told them that it was the sort of people their son knew that he was interested in, and not necessarily Aron Steinn himself, they asked no further questions and gave him the address. They did advise him to exercise a little caution and warned that some of Aron Steinn's friends were more repulsive than bohemian 'if he knew what they meant'. He didn't have a clue what they meant but thanked them anyway and accepted their condolences. If there was anything they could possibly do...

When he arrived at the address he thought he'd been given the wrong house number. Or the wrong street. The house was a beautiful single-level dwelling with a huge garage and a brand new Jeep parked out front along with two Harley Davidson motorcycles. He made his way up the driveway and reached out to knock but someone had seen him coming and the door magically swung open for him. The leather-clad woman who opened the door enquired as to what he wanted simply by raising one of her impressively groomed eyebrows.

'I'd like to see Aron Steinn, or Áskell.'

'Do you have a warrant, officer?'

'I'm not with the police. The boys know me.'

This statement was met with the raising of the same eyebrow all over again, although this time it lifted just a shade higher.

'I didn't say they liked me, just that they know me. I'm

Kjartan, Bella and Abelína's father. Can you just tell them I'm here and I need to talk to them? It's important.'

She looked him up and down one more time and closed the door in his face. There was a brief conversation he couldn't quite make out inside and then the door opened again. Aron Steinn stood before him in black jeans and a black singlet, all muscles and tattoos and not an ounce of self-doubt to be seen anywhere. He flicked both eyebrows simultaneously at Kjartan as a greeting but didn't say a word. If he ever moved to Reykjavík the first thing he would need to do was learn the sign-language.

'How are you doing, Aron Steinn?'

'I'm doing okay. I'm really sorry to hear about Bella, it's just been on the news.'

'They don't waste any time broadcasting bad news these days, do they? It hasn't been much of a day so far but I was wondering if you could help me. I thought if I could find out a few things it might make it easier to understand.'

Aron Steinn relaxed his stance a little so he didn't look quite so imposing. It wasn't much of a change though, he still resembled an attack dog on two legs.

'Sure.'

'After Bella ran away from home I assume you two would have been near the top of her list of places to visit. Am I right? After all, she didn't really know anyone else here so I'm assuming she would have looked to you guys for help.'

'She called me from Selfoss, she said she'd hitched that far and couldn't be bothered trying to get another lift so would I come pick her up.'

'And did you?'

'Sure, but I dropped her off in the city centre. She said she had no intention of living out here in the 'burbs. Apparently she had better things to do than hang out with us lowlifes.'

'And after that?'

'Not a thing. The next I heard about her was ten minutes ago on the television. Looks like she would have been better off out here with us after all.'

Kjartan looked down at his shoes and wondered again what could have driven her out of their home and into the arms of complete strangers. But he knew he had to steel himself against such moments of inward contemplation. For the time being, at least. This was a time for doing rather than for reflecting. There would be more than enough of that once he was back in Leirubakki with the shattered remains of his family.

'Look, do you want to come in and take a load off for a while?'

'No, I'll be okay in a minute, this is just all very difficult to take in. I saw her in the morgue this morning, the guy who killed her cut her face open like he was gutting a fish. What sort of a person would do something like that? What sorts of maniacs do we have running loose out there?'

'I don't know. This world takes all sorts.'

'I'm planning to stay in town for a couple of days until I find out what happened. I'm not convinced the cops know what they're doing and I want to see that whoever did this gets what he deserves. One way or another, if you know what I mean.'

'What are you saying? Just so we're clear here.'

'What I'm saying is that if I find this guy before they do

I'm going to make sure he never gets the chance to do this again to anyone else.'

Aron Steinn looked down both sides of his property to see if any of the neighbours were looking his way but the street was as quiet as it always was. He stepped out of the doorway and put his arms around Kjartan in a surprisingly affectionate hug. Kjartan trembled a little in the muscled giant's embrace as he whispered something in his ear.

'You find this guy and I'll put a bullet in the motherfucker's head for you. No questions asked. I loved that little chick like she was my sister.'

He slowly let go of Kjartan and wiggled a home-made business card into his jacket pocket.

'I mean it,' he said. 'Any time, day or night. I'm there.'

Kjartan nodded and patted his pocket.

'I know you do.'

'You just say the word.'

Aron Steinn turned around and walked back inside, closing the door behind him. Kjartan was left standing alone on the doorstep wondering what he was getting himself into and not really caring one way or the other. He realised now that he hated himself for not doing enough to prevent her death and he was determined to make up for it. He might not be able to bring her back but he could find who was responsible and even things up a little.

#6

GRÍMUR STOOD IN the middle of Gunnar Atli's living room with his hands on his hips. He hadn't noticed anything out of the ordinary on his first visit and wasn't sure if anything was going to jump out at him this time around either but he wanted a second look all the same. The place was tidy, very tidy for a single guy living on his own. There were no signs of any sort of disturbance, the place looked as it should and that was what worried him. For a guy who was having problems with his medication or lack thereof, there should have been more signs of chaos about the place. Any sign of chaos in fact.

Gunnar Atli had been reunited with his little pharmaceutical helpers now and was hopefully going to start remembering something helpful soon. He was going to be held until such time as the prosecutor saw fit to charge him or release him, which could be weeks, months or even years under Icelandic law. There was however a strong possibility that his lawyer would succeed in getting him transferred to Kleppspítali for observation rather than allowing him to be held in custody. He had seen the wheels turning in her head as soon as the subject of his medication and his previous stint in Klepp came up. For now though he was on his way to Litla Hraun to spend a while there. Grímur was hoping that his memory might improve a little while he was in prison, maybe even a lot.

Grímur turned to the one thing that had caught his eye the first time around. The framed photograph of Gunnar Atli and his ex-girlfriend, Nanna. He pulled an evidence bag from his back pocket and carefully took the photo out of its frame. It couldn't have been taken too long before the crash that had killed her and condemned Gunnar Atli to years of supervised hospitalisation. Whatever had happened, it must have been some crash.

For now though it was back to basics, all the neighbours who knew either the victim or the alleged attacker needed to be talked to again and even the ones who didn't. The uniformed officers had taken statements from several of them earlier but they had been fairly basic and hadn't focused on anything more complicated than what people had heard or seen throughout the night. For the most part that had been nothing even slightly out of the ordinary.

According to one of the statements there was a fairly alert neighbour directly downstairs from where Grímur was now. The guy's name was Davið Runar and he was a retired coast guard captain, a man of the sea. If anybody had spotted any odd behaviour around the place of late it would be him. It was a small and quiet street where anything strange would stand out a mile away to the eyes of an experienced navigator. He slipped the photo of the happy couple into his jacket pocket and made his way downstairs.

His first impressions of Davið Runar were pretty much as he'd expected they would be. Serious, smart as a whip and all business. The sort who wouldn't have taken any guff during his command on the high seas. He was immediately invited in for coffee and took a seat next to the window in the spotless living room while Davið Runar fixed their drinks in the kitchen. There was a framed insignia from the Icelandic coastguard on the wall with its anchor and chain symbol and its motto: Always Prepared. From the look of Davið Runar it would have been a surprise if too many things had ever caught him off guard in his time. The coffee was soon ready and poured into mugs and then Davið Runar signalled that he was ready for the questions to begin. He took seat directly opposite Grímur and looked him right in the eye.

'As you know there was a serious crime committed nearby last night. A girl's body was found outside your flat by the man who lives upstairs. Our officers were on the scene immediately because we received an anonymous tip-off but so far we haven't been able to trace the phone that was used to make the call. That wasn't you, was it?'

Davið Runar shook his head and smiled, a not unpleasant smile but serious nonetheless.

'I have no need for that level of secrecy. You would have found me waiting outside with the poor thing if I'd known anything of what was going on.'

'That's pretty much what I thought. Someone on this street made that call though and I need to know why they didn't leave a name and why we haven't been able to trace their phone.'

'Maybe they were just scared.'

'Afraid of whoever killed the girl?'

'Sure, if you were turning someone in who'd just done a thing like that you'd take as many precautions as you could too.'

'I guess I would.'

'Of course you would, you'd be an idiot otherwise.'

'Did you have much to do with your upstairs neighbour?'

'Not really, I was never a big fan of the guy. A few of the tenants here were opposed to him moving in here in the first place and I was one of them. I didn't mind him knowing that and I don't mind you knowing that either.'

'Why was that?'

'His stint in Kleppspítali put some of us off. We wouldn't be prejudiced against anyone with those sorts of problems but the guy spent a long time there and we were just concerned that he might not fit in. They have halfway houses for those sorts, you know? I was always of the opinion that he would have been better suited to one of those places.'

'Did the two of you ever talk about his time in

Kleppspítali?'

Davið Runar chuckled at the thought of that. His smile didn't last long though and he was soon back to looking serious again.

'I'm pretty sure he was aware of my opposition to him staying here from the very beginning so I don't know that he would have opened up to me even if I had asked. He probably thought he'd paid his dues, earned the right to an opportunity to fit back in. But I didn't agree with that. People like that bring baggage with them, sometimes an awful lot of it. He got himself a job of some kind and seemed to be keeping his nose clean but I always felt as if it was just a matter of time before something went wrong. Something always goes wrong, you see.

'You can prepare for every contingency in this life but there's always something that's going to catch you out. He might have done his best to work things through but that best might not have been good enough. No one has complete control over their own destiny and some people have a lot less control than others. Some know enough to swim with the current while others are so busy flapping about it's all they can do to not drown.'

'And he was a flapper?' Grímur asked with a trace of a smile on his lips.

'He was flapping when I first laid eyes on him and I bet he's still flapping now.'

Grímur struggled to wipe the smile from his face as he pictured the paranoid young man meeting the world weary sea-captain for the first time. He pulled the photo of Gunnar Atli and Nanna out of his jacket pocket and showed it to Davið Runar.

'Have you ever seen this girl before?'

'Is that the dead girl?'

'No, an old girlfriend of his from before his time in Kleppspítali.'

'Funny, she looks like the girl who used to visit him here until recently.'

'Who was that?'

'I wouldn't know her name but she looked like that girl there. Not exactly the same, just awfully similar. Used to argue with him all the time, the way some women like to. She stayed with him for about a week and then disappeared.'

'Did this girl have long dark hair like the one in the photo?'

'The first couple of times I saw her she did but after that she cut it short and dyed it.'

'Like she was going for a different look maybe?'

'Sure, or she was trying to hide from someone. It wasn't long after the thing with the hair that she moved in upstairs but like I said that only lasted a week and then she was gone.'

'And how long ago was that?'

'I haven't seen her in maybe four or five days.'

Grímur pulled out a picture of Bella that had been taken by Björn not long after her body had been found and handed it to Davið Runar. He studied it for a couple of seconds before handing it back without comment.

'Is that the girl you saw here?' Grímur asked.

'That's her, the one with the big mouth, only it's even bigger now. You see what I mean about the way they look alike?'

Grímur was pleased he wasn't the only one who had noted the similarity. He stood up and turned around so he could see out the front window. To get any sort of view at all he had to stand at the very end of the sofa or directly in front of it.

Either way his view was obscured by the ferns that grew just outside in the garden. There was no way that Davið Runar would have been able to see Bella where she had been hidden even if he'd known exactly where to look. Grímur thanked him for his time and told him that if he thought of anything else he should give him a call.

He was going to need another talk with Gunnar Atli, and sooner rather than later. It appeared that the reliability of his memory had been affected in all sorts of ways recently.

His next stop was the building where Bella had been living, just three doors up the street on the corner of Barónsstígur. He let himself into the building and went straight up to the first floor. When he let himself in with the keys Björn had given him he was instantly disappointed. Bella's flat was so clean it looked as if someone had been over it with a toothbrush. It no longer even looked as if someone had been staying there. There were no dirty dishes, no rubbish in the bin, the bed had been made up recently with clean sheets and her bags were packed and ready and waiting where she had left them on the living room floor. Something didn't feel right at all. If she had been in such a hurry to get away it seemed unlikely she would have gone to such an effort to clean the place. And if she'd been planning to leave all along then why hadn't she told anyone she was going? Or did she just never get the chance? It gave Grímur something else to ponder but wasn't making things any clearer for him at all. There was nothing for it but to keep going.

The door on the next floor up was answered by a tall thin lady with long jet-black hair and a crooked smile that didn't make her look happy. Grímur introduced himself and she nodded silently and let him in. She indicated that he should take a seat in one of her old-fashioned armchairs.

'I'm Adolfína, would you like some coffee?'

'No, thank you,' he replied. Davíð Runar's brew already had his synapses buzzing and snapping like a poorly wired fuse-board. The country's coastguard crews must like their coffee both hot and strong. He studied the woman in front of him as she glided into the kitchen. She looked somewhere over forty but it was hard to say exactly where. She was very handsome in a severe sort of way. Hard to read might have been the best way to describe her face. When she returned she had a tray of small delicious looking cakes in her hands. She placed it on the coffee table without a word and took a seat just across from him, so that she was not directly in front of him but not that far away either. Grímur eyed the cakes. They did look rather good but he resisted the urge to try one.

'I appreciate that you've already talked to some of our officers today. Is there anything you can tell me about Bella that might help me get a better idea of what she was doing here? Who she spent time with or what she did with herself in Reykjavík? We know next to nothing about why she chose to come here or what she did after she arrived. We're in the process of trying to clarify that as much as we can.'

'She'd only been here a few months so we didn't really know each other that well. But we saw each other about the place, mainly going up and down the stairs or in the laundry room.'

'Do you know what she did for work?'

'I haven't a clue I'm afraid.'

'Her flat looks as though it's been cleaned recently and all her belongings are packed up as if she was ready to leave. Did she mention anything to you about going anywhere?'

'No, she hadn't said anything about leaving. As far as I could tell she was happy here.'

'I understand that you used to be a psychiatric nurse.'

'That's right, why?'

'No reason.'

'You must have a reason. Otherwise you wouldn't have asked.'

Grímur decided that this mysterious creature was a lot savvier than she first appeared to be. Her dreamy laid-back exterior was just a front for a rather more tuned-in lady than he'd first anticipated.

'Do you know the other people who live downstairs? There wasn't anyone there when we called this morning.'

'There's two girls live down there. I'm afraid I don't know much about them. They're foreign I think and don't have much to say for themselves.'

'They're not Icelandic?'

'No, I don't know where they're from.'

'You wouldn't happen to know if they're around or not, would you? I'd like to speak to them today as well if I can.'

'I've no idea.'

'When was the last time you saw them?'

'Maybe two or three days ago.'

'So they might have gone away somewhere for a holiday?'

'Perhaps.'

Adolfína smoothed some invisible crease out of her skirt and smiled. It wasn't just hard to see what was going on behind her eyes, it was impossible. She crossed her legs and waited for him to continue.

'Okay, when you see them again will you let them know that I need to speak to them as soon as possible?'

'Certainly.'

'Where do you work now? Are you still in psychiatry?'

'No, I'm retired.'

Grímur nodded to himself as he made a note of that. She helped herself to one of her own cakes and passed the tray over to him.

'You really should try one of these, their awfully good.'

There was something about her that didn't add up. She didn't look old enough to be retired and he'd never heard of anyone making a fortune working as a nurse.

Grímur gave in to temptation and tried one of the smaller ones. She was right, it was really good.

#7

ALL GRÍMUR WANTED now was for one thing to go as it was supposed to but it was starting to look as if he was never going to get his wish. On top of that, any hopes he might have had about this being a straight forward case had now well and truly faded. Gunnar Atli had lied to his face about how well he'd known Bella and the woman who lived above her had left him scratching his head.

First things first though. He needed to talk to Gunnar Atli as soon as he could to find out why he'd lied. A quick phone call from headquarters put paid to that idea.

According to the receptionist at Hverfisgata, while Grímur had been out questioning the neighbours, Gunnar Atli suffered some sort of a fit or seizure. She was a little hazy on the details but en route to Litla Hraun he started beating his head against the walls and back door of the police van. By the time the officers realised what was going on and pulled over to restrain him, he'd done enough damage to himself to necessitate urgent medical attention.

They'd had to turn around straight away and bring him back to the city centre. Once his wounds were dressed and he'd been sedated, he was examined by a relief doctor. The stand-in physician had been covering for a sick colleague and probably hadn't counted on anyone like Gunnar Atli becoming part of his day. Rather than deal with what promised to be a rather tricky case he had readmitted him as fast as he could to his old home-away-from-home, Kleppspítali, in the hope that they might know what to do with him. Anything to get the guy off his hands. That had been almost an hour ago and yet nobody thought to inform Grímur as the drama had been unfolding.

The receptionist didn't seem to know why he hadn't been told about this earlier, either; apparently it all happened too quickly for anybody to remember how to use a phone. Now he faced the prospect of having to obtain permission from the head of admissions at the psychiatric hospital just to talk to him again. As far as he could tell, Gunnar Atli was either extremely crazy or extremely clever. Whichever it was, there wouldn't be any quick and easy way around the procedural nightmare that now lay ahead of him so he made his way over to the east side of the city centre near the container port, to enquire about his chances of talking to their new patient.

After being told to wait for the third time he decided to sit on a park bench out in the light snow and smoke a cigarette. The head of admissions at Kleppspítali was Thorgeir Alfreðsson, a slick-looking older gent who was the uncontested heavyweight doctor-in-charge at the hospital. He was in fact one of the most respected psychiatrists in the country who dealt almost exclusively with unhinged and potentially dangerous citizens deemed too risky to release back into the community. It made him an almost priceless possession for the hospital, as well as the nation, but he occasionally seemed to be every bit as crazy as some of his patients. It had been suggested by various co-workers that for every bit of goodness he had been able to get to rub off on those in his care, they had imbued him with just a little of their madness much in the way that pollen attaches to bees too busy to notice exactly which flowers they're bumping into.

Grímur contemplated this as he stubbed his cigarette out and wandered back into the reception area with his hands driven firmly into his jacket pockets. As he approached the desk yet again, the young bright-eyed girl on duty, Lilja Skaftadóttir, was waiting for him with his visitor pass in her hand. She handed it to him but wouldn't release her grip on the thing until she was convinced he was paying sufficient attention to what she had to say.

'This is conditional on a few things, Grímur. Thorgeir wanted me to explain them to you but since you're both big boys I don't see why he can't do that himself. You're to go up the stairs to the first floor to the last office on the left. It has his name on it.'

Grímur nodded repeatedly and slowly turned to make his way up the stairs that sat between reception and the dining room. He couldn't get the clip on his visitor's pass to attach to his shirt so he just stuffed it in a pocket. It wasn't as if there was anyone around to check it anyway. The old staircase creaked under his weight as he made his way up to the first floor.

The last door on the left was open and the doctor had his feet on his desk with a newspaper resting on his knees and a cup of coffee in his hand. He smiled calmly as if he'd been expecting company and motioned for Grímur to take a seat on the other side of the desk. His office window gave him a view over the grounds and right out to the bay.

'Coffee?'

'No, thank you.'

'Been one of those days, hasn't it?'

'I've had better. How about you?'

The doctor waved the question away as if it were about to land in his coffee and spread its legs in a death roll.

'When can I talk to Gunnar Atli?'

Thorgeir folded his newspaper up and put in on top of a pile of paperwork.

'Straight to the point, Grímur, that's what I like about you. So many people seem to prefer beating around the bush these days. We're dealing with a very troubled individual here. As you probably know this is not his first visit with us.'

'I am aware of that. What can you tell me about that first stint?'

'Well, he was brought here following a rather nasty car accident. The young lady he was travelling with was killed and he suffered a badly broken leg. He recovered from the injury in time and with rehabilitation was able to walk again albeit it with something of a limp. It was during the physical recuperation that the psychological problems began. He held himself responsible for her death. Even tried to take his own life on a couple of occasions.'

'Do you still consider him a danger to himself?'

'Shortly I will let you decide that for yourself. I don't know what you've been told but he has been exhibiting some fairly self-destructive behaviour today. We have him heavily sedated at the moment and I doubt very much that he will talk to you but it would be a good idea for you to at least observe his injuries.'

'When can I see him?'

'Well, there's no time like the present, is there?'

He put his coffee down on the table and rolled out of his chair onto his feet before walking over to his office window and staring out at the snowy day. He seemed to lose himself for a moment as he stood silently looking at the scene set out before him.

'There's a couple of things you need to keep in mind.'

'What are those?'

'Gunnar Atli is a patient now, no longer just another one of your suspects,' Thorgeir held his hand up to cut short any objections that Grímur may have been about to offer. 'No matter what you think he may have done you are going to have to wait until we see fit to release him to your custody once again. But it would appear that he is far from ready for that.

'We have him sedated for his own good so I will only allow you the briefest of visits. Anything he might say to you should be considered to be of no use to you for the purposes of your investigation. I warn you against attempting to question him in the state he's in. His lawyer has left me in no doubt that should you transgress in this area she will be down here to see to it that you have no further access to the boy.'

'The boy, as you call him, is thirty years of age and presently the sole suspect in a murder case. The victim was raped and tortured before being killed. This man may very well seem traumatised but that may be because he has killed a young woman and doesn't want to end up spending a large portion of his life in prison.'

Thorgeir turned to face Grímur again with a wary, part-amused, part-condescending smile on his face.

'If I decide that I don't feel like letting you see him again, you will not have access to him. Do you understand that? The only reason you are getting to see him now is because I'm feeling a little charitable but I can assure you that won't last.'

'Tell me something. When you kept him here for almost eight years, was it because you considered him to be a danger to himself or to others?'

The smile, such as it was, disappeared from Thorgeir's face so quickly you would have been forgiven for forgetting it was ever there.

'His room is on the next floor up at the southern end of the corridor. You will find an orderly waiting for you who has been instructed to give you two minutes in the room to observe and nothing else. Do not try his patience on the two minutes and don't forget any of the other advice you've already been given. Enjoy the rest of your day.'

'I'll do my best.'

Thorgeir gestured towards the door indicating that the detective had taken all the time out of his day that he was going to take. Grímur had to assume he had hit home with his last comment and left it at that.

The huge orderly at the southern end of the 2nd floor corridor definitely looked as though he wasn't going to allow Grímur to take any liberties with the restrictions Thorgeir had imposed on his visit. He very well may have been employed for his dimensions alone. He was not the sort of guy any of the patients would ever think about disobeying, or anyone else for that matter.

'Thorgeir's explained the rules to you, yeah?' he said through his neatly-groomed ginger beard.

'Two minutes,' Grímur said.

'Two minutes,' the giant reiterated holding up two sausage-like digits so there was absolutely no confusion.

He opened the door and indicated that Grímur should step inside. The room was much smaller than he'd anticipated and wouldn't have allowed for much movement even if Gunnar Atli had been able to get up out of bed. Thorgeir hadn't been kidding about the damage he'd sustained during his seizure or whatever it was they were calling it now. His face was not a pretty picture. He looked like he'd been set upon by a bunch of guys with knuckle dusters. He had a broken nose, two black eyes, one of them so badly swollen it would be staying shut for the foreseeable future, and so many cuts and contusions on his face it was almost impossible to count. He looked surprisingly similar to the way Bella had when he'd found her, minus the grotesque cuts to her face. Whether or not that was merely coincidental was yet to be seen. He was lying perfectly still and seemed to be asleep.

If he'd been trying to keep himself out of prison he had definitely achieved that objective but in doing so had opened wide a window to the darker recesses of his mind, and it was within those soulless voids that the answer to Bella's death undoubtedly lay. All Grímur had to do now was get him to offer it up.

He stood over Gunnar Atli's prone figure and wondered why he had even bothered coming. He supposed that it was because he had needed to see what had happened for himself. Well, he had seen it with his own eyes now and he could go back and report to the powers that be in the prosecutor's office that they wouldn't be interviewing their prime suspect anytime soon.

Just as Grímur was turning to tell the red-headed giant he could lock up again and apologise for wasting his time he saw Gunnar Atli's lips move, so faintly that at first he thought he'd imagined it.

'Has he said anything to you since he was brought in?'

'He hasn't said a word. I don't even know if he can talk with his face all busted up like that. If you're waiting to have a conversation with him, you could be waiting a while.'

He had a good point. The fact that Gunnar Atli's jaw wasn't broken had to be down to luck and nothing else. That being said though, his lips continued to move almost imperceptibly as if reciting a silent prayer. Grímur knelt down and got his head as close to Gunnar Atli's mouth as he possibly could.

'Don't you go touching him or I'll have to throw you

out.'

The orderly definitely didn't sound as if he were joking. Grímur ignored him anyway and whispered softly to the sleeping patient.

'What is it? What are you trying to say?'

A sound escaped his lips, so faint Grímur wouldn't have heard it had he been six inches further away.

'We all learn to live with our mistakes.'

Grímur asked him to repeat himself a couple of times but to no avail. Gunnar Atli had drifted off back to wherever it was he had disappeared to. Whatever the name of that mysterious land he seemed destined to be spending plenty of time there in the near future. A thudding tap on his shoulder reminded him that his two minutes was up and it was time to go.

#8

IT WASN'T HARD for Kjartan to find the place where his daughter had been killed. The television news had shown the back of the city's church, Hallgrímskirkja, and from there he could see the street that had been closed off by the police. Leifsgata had been taped from one side to the other with black and yellow Lögreglan crime scene tape and only people who lived on the street were being allowed through. Because of the police presence most of the residents had been awake since the crack of dawn, at their windows or in their front gardens watching forensic and technical crews come and go.

As determined as he was, Kjartan stood absolutely no chance of getting close to where his daughter's body had been found. Along with the police at either end of the street, there were two more directly outside the apartment building. A polite but brief conversation with one of the officers at the top of the street extinguished any hopes he had of talking to her neighbours. Unless they wandered out of their homes and decided to speak to him of their own free will that just wasn't going to happen either.

There was another apartment block at the top end of Leifsgata – on the corner where it met Barónsstígur – that was also receiving some attention from forensic officers but not nearly as much as the one where Bella had been found. A little guess work and an hour or so of quiet observation from his car and Kjartan decided that this had to be the building where Bella had been living. As the day wore on and the police line slowly fell back he saw that he would probably be able to go for a wander as long as he didn't make a nuisance of himself. Eventually he spotted a couple of women entering the ground floor apartment of the corner building and decided the time was right to make his move.

He strolled across the road to the front of the building. The entrance to their flat wasn't up the steps and through the front door but through a private entrance just off the street in a small slightly overgrown garden. Very conscious that there might be eyes on him he casually knocked on the door and waited for an answer. The two of them had to be inside somewhere but there was only silence from within. He knocked again and this time heard tiny sounds of movement. The door opened no more than six inches and one of the women peered out at him. She was somewhere in her late twenties or early thirties and looked flustered and anxious to be left alone. As he opened his mouth to apologise for disturbing her she started shaking her head violently.

'No, I am sorry but today no good.' She spoke in hesitant English with a heavy Eastern European accent.

He understood now why they had seemed so nervous. He couldn't be sure but suspected they were in the country illegally. Her nervousness certainly seemed to suggest that this was the case. The woman was just about to shut the door in his face when she seemed to have a change of heart. She shoved him out of the way and looked hesitantly up and down the street as if trying to get a feel for who might be watching. Satisfied that they weren't being spied on she grabbed Kjartan by the jacket and pulled him into the flat in such a way that he didn't get a chance to argue. Once inside she closed the door again and turned towards him with an awkward smile on her face. The flat was tiny and barely had enough room for the two of them without adding him to the mix. She motioned to the two-seater sofa up against one of the walls and waited impatiently for him to sit down.

'Okay, sorry for that. I need your help for something,' she said.

She smiled again as he sat down as if to indicate that everything was going to be okay. Once he was sitting she nodded again before continuing.

'Something happen today? What?'

Kjartan realised that they had almost definitely seen

something on the news but weren't quite sure about what had actually happened, probably because whatever they had seen and heard had been on television and in Icelandic.

'A girl was murdered,' he said in his own out of practice English. 'Just down the street.' He tried pointing towards where the police were stationed hoping they would get the idea. The two women looked at each other and shared a brief conversation in their own language.

'Dead?'

'Yes, dead.'

'Why? No, who?'

'A girl, Bella. Perhaps you knew her?'

Kjartan pulled a photo of his daughter out of his wallet and showed it to the two women. There was a sudden intake of breath from both of them as they crossed themselves in rapid succession.

'My God,' the older one said.

The younger, prettier one still hadn't said a word.

'Do you know her?' he tried, hoping that the looks of recognition on their faces meant that he had finally got somewhere.

'Of course, she live here,' the older of the two said pointing at the ceiling.

'She lived upstairs?' he said.

'Yes, upstairs. Bella, yes.'

'Yes, Bella is her name. I am her father,' he said, pointing to himself.

Again the two of them conferred in their own language, the tone very serious this time. When they were done she pointed at him.

'You father?'

He just nodded solemnly this time. She crossed herself again and walked towards him. She wrapped her arms around him and hugged him whispering something foreign but gentle in his ear.

'Thank you,' he said in Icelandic, reverting momentarily to his mother tongue.

When she'd disentangled herself from him he motioned for her to sit down next to him.

'How well did you know Bella?'

'We, little bit, sorry,' she said, probably apologising for her poor English.

'How long did she live upstairs?'

'Maybe,' she seemed to be doing some arithmetic in her head, 'five months.'

'Five months, okay. So she must have been working somewhere then. Do you know where she worked?'

The two of them looked at each other and shrugged.

'Same as us,' she said with an expression that he couldn't quite figure out.

It might have been confusion but he wasn't sure.

'Same as you? Where do you two work?'

'Here. We thought you first customer today.'

She let that sink in. They both looked at him wondering if the penny had dropped yet or not.

'You mean, you two, and Bella?'

'Yes, we are whores,' she said without a trace of embarrassment or self-consciousness.

'And Bella too?'

She nodded and looked around the room as if unsure if she was breaking any previous confidences she'd agreed to keep. Kjartan exhaled from the bottom of his lungs as he took a moment to let that sink in. When he noticed that he was still holding her picture he carefully put it back in his wallet. Maybe that was something he would keep from the rest of the family. He wasn't convinced that knowing everything about her time in Reykjavík would make things any easier for Abelína or Helga to understand. There was a point where extra information ceased to be of any further use. That she was dead was probably enough for them to digest at the moment and for now he would let them remember her the way she had been before. Whatever she had become since leaving home was neither here nor there for the purposes of finding a lasting memory to hold onto. The way she was to be remembered over the next few days would be the way they would always remember her.

'Thank you,' he said again. 'What are your names?'

'Petra, and Dinka,' she said indicating that she was Petra and that the younger silent one was Dinka.

'I'm Kjartan. Thank you very much for talking to me.'

'You don't tell police about us?' She waved her arms around indicating everything in their flat, probably everything they had in their entire lives. Kjartan shook his head.

'No, I won't tell the police about you.'

'Thank you,' she said.

Kjartan smiled despite the awkwardness of the situation or maybe because of it. He had found out more about Bella than he'd bargained for but was still no closer to knowing what had happened to her. She had obviously run out of money and rather than asking her family for help she had sought to make up the shortfall by sleeping with strangers. The thought made him wonder what could have made her hate them so much, or care so little about herself.

'Just before I go, I was wondering. Did Bella know anyone else around here?'

Petra and Dinka looked at each other for a second or two until Petra spoke for them again.

'Gunnar Atli.'

'Gunnar Atli? Who is Gunnar Atli?'

Petra motioned outside and Kjartan put two and two together pretty quickly.

'The guy who lives down the street?'

'Yes, boyfriend.'

'Her boyfriend? What does her boyfriend look like?'

Petra indicated that he probably stood about 5' 8", had short hair of some kind and walked with a limp. Kjartan now had a clear picture in his mind of the man he needed to find.

#9

AS KJARTAN WANDERED back to his car a woman appeared out of the main door of the apartment building he'd just left. She was tall and thin with jet black hair and walked with real confidence and authority. She gave the street a cursory inspection before letting herself into Petra and Dinka's flat. He stopped where he was on the other side of the street and waited to see if she was going to stay or was just visiting the girls. He only had to wait a few minutes before he got his answer. She reappeared looking pensive and rubbing her arms to warm herself against the cold day.

As soon as she saw him making his way across the street towards her she snapped herself out of her reverie and regained her air of impregnability.

'Hello,' he said.

She smiled but it looked a little forced to say the least. She didn't reply but simply waited for him to state his business and get on with it.

'I was wondering if I could have a word with you. I'm Bella's father, Kjartan.'

That softened her up a little, but not much. She extended a long graceful arm and waited for him to take her hand.

'I'm Adolfína, I'm sorry to hear about your daughter. I don't really know what to say, it must be a dreadful time for you.'

'It is very difficult. We're struggling to believe it's really happened. I don't think anything can prepare you for news like that.'

'No, I can't imagine anything could. It must have come as such a shock. Is there anything I can do for you?'

'I was just hoping that I might be able to ask you a few questions. Would that be alright?'

'Of course.'

'She'd been here for a few months so you must have known her a little then?'

'Yes, she lived in the flat underneath mine. We would say hello to each other when we met but we weren't exactly close. I'm not sure that I'll be able to tell you all that much. Perhaps you would like to come in out of the cold? I could find something for us to eat and make us some coffee.'

'Yes, that would be nice,' he said.

She pulled a bunch of keys from her pocket and let them into the building. When they got up to the first floor she stopped and turned to look at him with her cold, pale blue eyes.

'The police have already been by to look at her flat. I'm afraid they've sealed it off until they finish their investigation. There isn't much to look at in there anyway. By the look of things she was all packed and ready to go somewhere but I haven't a clue where.'

'She hadn't mentioned anything to you about where she might have been planning to go? Did she mention Leirubakki to you by any chance?'

'No, I don't believe she did. Is that where you're from?'

'Yes, that's where she grew up.'

When Adolfína stepped onto the landing Kjartan could see that the door to his daughter's flat was sealed off with crime scene tape.

'I don't mean to be presumptuous but I'm assuming that you hadn't seen your daughter in some time,' Adolfína said.

'No, she ran off about six months ago and since then there's only been the occasional phone call. We're still at a loss as to why she left in the first place.'

'Come upstairs and I'll get us something to drink. You look like you could do with putting your feet up for a while. Times like these can be extremely tiring and you may not realise how worn out you really are, emotionally as well as physically.'

Kjartan nodded and followed her up another flight of stairs to the door of her own apartment. Adolfína's flat was warm and cosy, it had a lived-in sort of look about it as though she'd been there for some time and was very settled. She was right about how exhausted he was but his mind didn't want to listen to what his body was trying so hard to tell it. While he took a seat in one of her plush armchairs she busied herself in the kitchen making coffee and arranging a plate of smoked lamb for them to share. He was soon filling himself with the strong coffee and slices of hangikjöt and rye bread and starting to feel revived again. Adolfína sipped her coffee but only ate a little. She had the figure of a bird and the appetite of one too.

'I really appreciate this, I haven't had anything to eat today. It's all been such a shock. I only came to identify her body but now I've decided to stick around for a couple of days,' he said.

'Whatever for? Surely you'd be better off in Leirubakki with your family?'

'I won't be heading home. Not until they've released her body and I've seen that the man who did this to her is brought to justice. It's important for me to see that the right thing is done. Otherwise we won't be able to lay her to rest properly.'

'Do they think they know who did it then?'

'They've arrested a guy who lives just down the street. He was found with her body when the police arrived but he insists he had nothing to do with it.'

'And you don't believe him?'

'Of course not, would you? I think he had help though, and now his partner's disappeared. He's pretending to be crazy so he doesn't go to prison. Apparently he's made up some ridiculous story about not being able to remember what happened. Memory loss of some sort. People do that sort of thing you know. When it looks like someone's going to jail they'll do just about anything to save themselves.'

'So you think there's more than one guy behind it?'

'Even the police think so but they're not saying much else at the moment. They have this guy in custody yet they seem pretty reluctant to point the finger at him. I suppose no one wants to look stupid when you're dealing with something like this. If you were to get it wrong you'd never live it down, would you?'

'No, I don't suppose you would. Are you sure you want to be concerning yourself with these things so soon after her death? Don't you think it might be a better idea to allow yourself some time?'

'There'll be time enough when I've got her back home where she belongs. Right now I intend to see to it that the police do their job. I know what they're like. The whole system's too easy on people who commit these sorts of crimes. It's not just the police, it's the courts as well. They get off too easy. I'm determined to see that there's absolutely no chance of that happening this time.'

'But what are you planning to do?'

'First of all I'm going to find out as much as I can about this guy they've arrested. I want to know everything there is to know about him.'

'You know who it is then?'

'He lives down the street where those cops are standing around talking to each other and he's called Gunnar Atli. I don't suppose you know who I'm talking about?'

'Yes, he lives three doors down and works at the hospital.'

'Landspítali?'

'Yes, he works in the kitchen there.'

'How well do you know him?'

'I was a nurse at Klepp, he used to be a patient there.'

'Kleppspítali? So it's possible he's not making up all this stuff about memory loss?'

'I can't talk about the specifics but I don't think memory loss was ever an issue.'

'What do you mean?'

'From what I recall, most of his problems didn't come from a lack of memories but rather from dealing with the memories of the accident.'

'Accident? What sort of accident are we talking about?'

'A car accident. He and his girlfriend were involved in a car accident and she was killed. He took it rather badly. I think he blamed himself for what happened and tried to kill himself. That was why he was placed in our care.'

'So Bella's the second girlfriend of his to wind up dead and he's got a history of mental illness? A smart lawyer would argue that he should have never been released in the first place. That he should go back there rather than to Litla Hraun.'

'It's possible. You know, I still have some friends at Klepp. I could give someone a call and find out if they've heard anything. It would only take a moment and it might make you feel better.'

'I'd be very grateful. That might help put my mind at rest.'

'I don't mind at all, just give me a couple of minutes and I'll see what I can find out.'

Adolfína went to her bedroom to find her phone. She

scrolled through her contacts until she found the number she was looking for and didn't have to wait long for it to be answered.

'Hi, it's me. I've got the murdered girl's father here with me ... That's right, he is rather upset... He's looking for information about Gunnar Atli. Is there anything you can tell me that I can pass onto him?'

Adolfína listened intently for a few minutes without speaking.

'No problem, anything else? ... Thanks very much, I'll let him know.'

Adolfína walked back out to Kjartan and smiled.

#10

GRÍMUR STEPPED OUT of the heavy snow and in through the front door of police headquarters on Hverfisgata, absent-mindedly wiping white sludge from his sleeves as he went. He'd found his trip to Klepp more disturbing than productive. Between the arrogant Thorgeir Alfreðsson and the almost unconscious yet still mumbling Gunnar Atli all he could see were problems mounting at every turn when it came to orchestrating a prosecution. For the time being the man was considered to be a serious danger to himself and wasn't going anywhere. He hadn't a clue what he'd meant by 'We all learn to live with our mistakes'. Maybe it had finally hit home that he'd made one too many errors of judgment and that there was no way back for him this time. Maybe it didn't mean anything at all.

A pile of paper work had grown on his desk in his brief absence. There were notes requesting interviews with newspapers and television stations all of which he threw straight in the bin. He was in no mood for explaining his day to anyone if he didn't absolutely have to. They would manage to get their sound bites and quotes from someone else. They always did. The rest of the pile looked like what he had asked for earlier in the morning. There were records concerning Gunnar Atli's employment, driving record, tax payments, phone bills, medical history, etc. He had sent a couple of officers to Leirubakki to interview the rest of the family as well. A thankless task considering what they would be going through today but it had to be done. They had been told to bring back anything that might be considered of interest and even some things that might not. He knew from previous experience that it could be the smallest detail that would bring them success and that the most important part of discovering who was responsible for her death was finding out who might have wanted her dead in the first place.

He fingered the pieces of paper one by one, setting them aside into separate piles according to their degree of interest to him. They probably weren't going to teach him much he didn't already know but with Gunnar Atli locked away in the puzzle factory for the foreseeable future he was a little short on ideas as to exactly how they should proceed.

Gunnar Atli's driving record was relatively clean apart from the accident that had killed his girlfriend. Before that there had been a couple of speeding tickets but that was it and there was no sign he had owned a vehicle since. He had been in hospitals of one kind or another for eight of the nine years since then so that was no real surprise. After an ordeal like that Grímur doubted if he would have had the stomach to get behind the wheel again either.

He had worked part-time before the accident delivering for a bakery in Reykjavík. The job had helped him through university where he earned a degree in Environmental Science. That was presumably where he met girlfriend number one, Nanna. His medical record up until the accident had been completely inconsequential, the broken leg he'd suffered in the crash being the only physical trauma of any consequence he'd ever suffered. It consisted of five breaks to his right leg, all below the knee and his right ankle had been rebuilt with pins and screws as a result. Apparently he had been lucky not to lose the lower part of his leg.

His psychiatric records wouldn't be released without a court order and even then it would be a prolonged battle if Thorgeir Alfreðsson didn't feel like handing them over, which he probably wouldn't. That was a shame because it was almost undoubtedly in those files that the key to this mystery lay. As for Bella, her life had been far less colourful, until recently that was. Murder had a way of spicing up a person's profile where before there had only been drab and mundane events. The girl had endured a colourless time at school, had no medical problems of any note and had never been so much as pulled over while driving. Something had caused her to run away from home and never look back, though.

A note had been left on one of the interview sheets about a remark made by a friend of the family. Apparently Bella had been regarded as something of a tramp around her hometown of Leirubakki. He hadn't elaborated on what that might have had to do with her disappearance but otherwise there didn't seem to be any clues to explain why she'd wanted out of the place so badly. It was possible that something had happened at or after the wedding. They were now in the process of tracking down and interviewing every single guest but that would take time. Maybe she just hadn't been able to handle all the attention her sister had received and realised that it was never going to happen for her. Not if she stayed where she was, anyway.

One of the officers included something that caught Grímur's eye. It was the sister's wedding certificate, Abelína Kjartansdóttir. Grímur couldn't for the life of him think why a wedding certificate would be pertinent to a murder investigation but he had learned the hard way not to ignore anything, no matter how small and unconnected it seemed. In a case with virtually no leads apart from a crazy man in a hospital bed it would be unwise to dismiss anything and his instructions to 'bring me copies of absolutely everything' had been unequivocal.

He ran his eyes over the certificate. There wasn't all that much in the way of information on it. The names and signatures of the couple getting married, the minister who had presided over the ceremony, and the witnesses, all no doubt friends of the bride and groom. The officer who copied the certificate had ringed the name of one of the witnesses with a black pen and made a small note next to it - 'Also disappeared after the wedding but now back in Reykjavík, as of December 23rd.' The name of the witness was Viveca Thorgeirsdóttir and the address was in the city centre not far from Leifsgata. Her name was certainly interesting. Viveca Thorgeirsdóttir; it was definitely worth checking out.

If her father was the same Thorgeir as Gunnar Atli's doctor it was too much of a coincidence to ignore. Even if he wasn't, it was still something. But not much. Considering the lack of any other real leads they had to go on, it was worth following up. He grabbed his keys.

The house was on the expensive-looking side of things. An old two-storey wooden home with a large double-garage attached. The garage door was open and there were empty spaces for two cars. It was probably safe to assume that they were out somewhere but he decided it was worth a try anyway now that he was there. When he rang the doorbell a thin, very pretty blonde girl in her twenties answered the door and asked what he wanted.

'Are you Viveca?'

She smiled at him in a way that suggested she was bored and his unexpected appearance at her front door was just the distraction she'd been looking for.

'I am, and who might you be?'

'My name is Grímur, I'm a police officer. Are either of your parents home?'

'No. Dad's been called in to work and Mum's, I don't know, out I guess.'

'Okay, I'd like to ask you some questions. I believe you were at a wedding in Leirubakki about six months ago. Is that correct?'

'Yeah, how did you know?'

'Do you remember if your friend Abelína had a sister? Or rather, did you meet her sister?'

'Yeah, I did. She introduced herself right as I was leaving. She was pretty wasted by then. She didn't get herself in any trouble did she?'

'She was found dead this morning, you may have seen it on the news.'

'That was her?'

'That was her.'

'Oh my God.'

'Did you have any contact with her after the wedding? See her again, talk to her on the phone, maybe?'

'She said she was thinking about moving to Reykjavík and that she wanted to catch up when she got here so she'd at least know someone.'

'And did you?'

'What?'

'Catch up with her?

'No, she called here to see me not long after the wedding but by then I'd had a fight with Dad and wasn't around. I took off with my boyfriend to Akureyri for a few months. Sometimes you just have to get away, you know?'

'So your parents met her while you were away?'

'Mum did, I don't know about Dad.'

'I'd like to talk to both of them, are they expected home soon?'

'To be honest I don't really know. Mum's at a friend's place I think. She'll be drunk and probably won't be back for a while. And Dad's at work, he's a psychiatrist. He was called into work on his day off to deal with some loony.'

Grímur had never been much of a believer in coincidences.

#11

WHAT ADOLFÍNA TOLD him hadn't come as too much of a surprise. Kjartan'd had a bad feeling all along that Gunnar Atli would play on his psychiatric history to avoid spending any time in prison and now his suspicions had been confirmed. With his prior psychiatric record he stood a good chance of being taken seriously as a genuine nutcase, even if all he'd done was beat himself up in the back of a police van.

That could not be allowed to happen.

In the middle of winter Kleppspítali was at its most

beautiful and serene. Stands of naked Icelandic birch
graced the grounds along with some of the city's most
luxurious fir trees. The red corrugated iron roof was
almost completely covered with white powder matching
the ivory carpet that lay all around the majestic old
building.

Rather than drive into the car park Kjartan parked
some distance away and walked. Lilja Skaftadóttir greeted
him at the front door where she stood alongside what had
to be one of the orderlies or security personnel. Lilja was in
her mid-twenties, blond and chirpy-looking while the guy
with her was the best part of 6'7" and looked like he was
eyeing Kjartan up for lunch.

'Hi there,' Lilja chirruped.

The red-headed behemoth smoking a cigarette beside
her nodded to acknowledge he'd seen Kjartan but nothing
more. Kjartan pulled out a notebook and pretended to
check a few details in it before addressing Lilja.

'I understand you had a man by the name of Gunnar
Atli Davíðsson admitted here today,' he said. 'I was
wondering if we might have a talk about him if that's all
right with you. It won't take long.'

'We're not supposed to discuss patients with members
of the public, sorry,' Lilja stated.

'Of course. It's just that his being here is something the
public deserve to know about, don't you think? I was
wondering if there was someone here I could get a
statement from regarding his admission, considering he's a
suspect in a murder case. That's something I'm sure our
readers would be interested in.'

Kjartan smiled but it was the smile of a man

determined to be a pain in the arse rather than a genuine attempt to be pleasant. Lilja and the orderly looked at each other as if they were waiting for one another to come up with a solution then Lilja got up on her toes and whispered something in her colleague's ear. He thought about what she said for a second and then nodded before turning on his heels and disappearing into the building. Lilja stared hard at the cigarette in her hand and seemed to be doing a great deal of thinking about something.

'We're going to see if anyone feels like talking to you,' she said.

'Thank you, I appreciate it.'

Lilja was obviously toying with the idea of saying more but seemed to be undecided on whether to speak her mind or not. She sucked on her cigarette instead and pulled her cardigan a little tighter around her shoulders.

'He's the guy who killed that girl this morning, isn't he? We're not allowed to watch television in here but my friends have been messaging me, saying that he's the one they're all talking about on the news today,' she said.

'Yes, he is. That's why I want to speak to someone for a comment about why he's here. Some people think he should be locked up someplace more secure. That he's just faking his condition to avoid spending time in prison.'

'I don't know anything about that,' she said.

The cheerfulness had left her voice though and been replaced with something more thoughtful and considered. As she stubbed out her cigarette a man appeared beside her at the door and gently placed his hand on her shoulder.

'Is this the gentleman, Lilja?'

'Yes, this is him,' she said and instantly disappeared

behind him back into the building.

'My name is Thorgeir, how may I help you?'

'I was wondering if you'd like to make a comment on the presence of Gunnar Atli Davíðsson at your facility.'

'If you're looking for me to discuss the details of a patient here you should know that I can't do that.'

'Okay, would it be safe to assume that there is a patient here who was brought in today because he is considered to be a danger to himself?'

Kjartan didn't wait for an answer he knew wasn't coming. Thorgeir continued to stand in front of him with his arms crossed looking both condescending and vaguely amused at the same time.

'Don't you think he would be better suited to a more secure facility where he could be properly detained in the interest of public safety since it is in fact them and not himself that he is a threat to?'

This time there was a real smile from Thorgeir.

'May I ask what your name is and which media source it is you represent?'

'My name is Kjartan Jónsson and I represent myself and my family. I represent Ísabella Kjartansdóttir because no one else is going to if I don't. She died at the hands of this maniac and all I see now is people concerning themselves with his wellbeing.'

Kjartan took a quick couple of steps towards Thorgeir but stopped just short of making any physical contact with him.

'What I want to know,' Kjartan raised a finger and held it just in front of Thorgeir's face, trembling with the self-control needed to hold himself back from attacking him. 'Is who's worried about what happened to her?'

Thorgeir took a full step back from Kjartan and took a moment to formulate his reply. He looked around the grounds to see if anyone else may have heard Kjartan's outburst.

'I strongly suggest you go home, Kjartan, before someone takes an idea to call the police. You're not doing anyone any good by coming here, you need to grieve for your loss instead of wasting precious time venting your anger on strangers. Behaving this way isn't going to help you or your family.'

'If you help him to stay here instead of going to prison where he belongs, I'll be back.'

Thorgeir took a step out of the doorway towards Kjartan and stared down his nose at him.

'You're not threatening me are you?'

Thorgeir turned his head slightly and whispered something to someone waiting behind him who Kjartan couldn't quite see.

'I really think it is time for you to go now.'

'Make sure he's out of here as soon as possible or else he's going to have even more to worry about than he does right now. You can tell him that I know what he's playing at and that I know he can't hide here forever. Sooner or later he's going to be out and I'll be waiting for him. Someone needs to be held accountable for what happened to Bella and right now he's the only one who can answer my questions about what happened to her. Either he admits what he did or he tells us who killed her.'

'I advise you to leave now before the police arrive, I understand Lilja has already called them for me. It is not for the likes of us to make such decisions. If someone needs to be evaluated for the good of their own psychological health, well, that's what we're here for. We can't operate this hospital with patients under threat of physical violence or worse, it just won't work that way. You must try to understand that.'

In the distance a siren sounded as if to reiterate the impending arrival of the authorities. Kjartan shuffled his feet in the snow and gathered his thoughts, he was in no great hurry to leave just yet.

'If that had been your daughter and you'd had to look at her as she lay on that cold metal table, all cut up and broken beyond repair, then what? If that had been you instead of me, tell me, what would you want to do?'

'I would want to find the man responsible, of course, but I would pray for justice to be done rather than attempt to take the law into my own hands. Men like Gunnar Atli are destined to be judged by a higher law than you or I. Be careful not to confuse yourself with Him.

'For with the judgment you pronounce you will be judged, and with the measure you use it will be measured to you. Time for you to go, please remember what I have told you.'

The police siren had stopped nearby but no officers were visible just yet. Kjartan could hear voices and footsteps approaching though. He turned and disappeared slowly through the snow-covered grounds, with Thorgeir's advice ringing in his ears.

#12

GRÍMUR RECEIVED THE call at 8 o'clock the next morning. Thorgeir and his wife Renata had agreed to talk to him although the meeting had been set up through their daughter, Viveca. The fact that at least one of them had met Bella when she first arrived in Reykjavík was of interest to him. He didn't know of anyone else she'd met other than her upstairs neighbour, Adolfína and the man who may just have killed her, Gunnar Atli. It was possible she had dropped a clue of some sort as to why she'd left Leirubakki in such a hurry. Of course she may not have mentioned it at all but still, he had to try. It was going to be hard to unravel the story of what she'd been doing with herself unless he could find people who had met her no matter how fleeting their interactions had been.

He arrived at the house at 9 o'clock sharp and when Viveca welcomed him he could tell straight away she wasn't as perky as she had been the previous day. He put it down to the fact that her parents were both back in the house and decided that while he had her to himself in the living room for a minute or two he would ask her a few quick questions.

'Tell me more about Bella at the wedding. Her family say they don't know why she would have run away but you know how families are. Sometimes they can't see what's going on even when it's right under their noses.'

'Tell me about it. I really don't remember too much about her that night to be honest. I think Abelína had told her to introduce herself to me so she'd know someone when she got to town and so we had a bit of a chat. I gave her my number and address but I was kind of halfway out the door at that stage and she was pretty trashed, so I kept it quick rather than spend half an hour talking about a load of rubbish. You know how people get at that time of the night.'

'Sure, did she call you after that?'

'I got a few missed calls from her when I got back from the wedding but I'd had a pretty big fight with my parents and didn't answer my phone for about a week after that. She must have given up trying to call and just come looking for me instead.'

'What was the fight about?'

'Same old shit. I don't appreciate anything they've done for me, bla, bla, bla and just because they're adoptive parents doesn't mean I shouldn't have the same respect for them as real parents, bla, bla, bla. Like I said, same old shit that we've been arguing about for years.'

'You're adopted? How old were you when that happened?'

'Five.'

'So they're all you've ever known then?'

'Pretty much. My real mum died when I was small so I don't remember her and Dad was never around.'

'Do Thorgeir and Renata have any other children?'

'They had a son, Anders but he died really young. They don't like talking about it very much. After that happened they tried to have another kid but just couldn't for some reason. That's when I came into it, I guess. Lucky old last resort, that's me.' She giggled a little when she said that. 'I shouldn't be ungrateful but everything would be a hell of a lot easier if they'd just chill out a bit. Sometimes I think they go out of their way to drive me crazy.'

Grímur smiled to himself as Thorgeir and Renata made their way into the living room with cups of coffee for everyone. Thorgeir took a seat opposite Grímur as Renata passed coffee cups around. He looked anxious to get the meeting over with.

Viveca moved to a seat a little further away as she tried to blend into the background. Her plan seemed to work well as Thorgeir instinctively took centre-stage.

'Nice to see you again, Grímur. Have you many questions for us? Unfortunately we both have rather busy days ahead.'

'That suits me fine, I'll get right to it,' Grímur said as he opened his notebook.

'We don't mean to rush you, it's just we've an awful lot on our plate,' Renata added.

Grímur could understand how Viveca struggled on occasion to deal with the two of them and how disagreements could end up with her walking out of the house. There was something phoney and thoroughly irritating about both of them. When they'd discovered they weren't able to have any more children the news must have come as something of an embarrassment. Viveca had probably been taken on board as a quick-fire solution and had slowly grown unhappy with her ceremonial place in the family. He glanced in her direction but she was messaging someone on her phone.

'That's quite all right, I'm a reasonably busy man myself. What I wanted to talk to you about was when Bella came here looking for Viveca. I need to know a few things; what she said, how she looked, that kind of thing. Anything at all that you can remember might be useful. I'm trying to piece together what she did with herself once she got to Reykjavík, as well as why she left Leirubakki in the first place. Did she give a specific reason why she wanted to see Viveca or do you think it was just a social visit?'

Thorgeir gestured towards his wife as if to suggest that she should be the one to field that question. She looked sideways at Grímur and fidgeted with her coffee cup a little before answering.

'She didn't say exactly why she wanted to see Viveca. Just that they'd arranged to meet up with each other. I told her that while it sounded like a lovely idea, Viveca had taken us all by surprise and run off with that dreadful boyfriend of hers. She has a terrible habit of doing that when things don't go her way. Haven't you, dear?'

She turned to see if her daughter was going to respond but Viveca was too busy with her phone to notice anyone else. Renata turned back to Grímur and shrugged as if to say there was only so much she could do with what she'd been given.

'She didn't mention anything about why she'd come here in the first place?'

'Nothing at all, I thought she might have been looking for somewhere to stay but all she asked about was Viveca and when I told her we hadn't the faintest idea where she was, she just left. I'm afraid I can't really be of any more help to you.'

Thorgeir cleared his throat to get everyone's attention as he straightened his tie and finished his coffee.

'If the girl fell in with a bad crowd here in Reykjavik I think you can safely assume it had very little to do with her visit here. I'm no expert on such matters but I would have thought the people she spent time with just before she died would be of more interest to you than those she met in this house,' Thorgeir said.

'Thank you for the observation, Thorgeir. As we both know, the person who best fits that description is presently resting in one of your hospital beds. If he were available for questioning it is more than likely I wouldn't be wasting your valuable time. It's important we cross everyone she had contact with off our list, otherwise we wouldn't be doing our jobs properly. Thank you both for your time though, I'll leave you now to get on with your day.'

'Our pleasure, Viveca will show you out,' Thorgeir said as he got up and left the room.

There was something about the guy that was just too smug. He was really full of himself. Viveca got up and walked him to the door still holding onto her phone but looking a little more relaxed now that Thorgeir was out of the room. It had started to snow again but it was much lighter than the day before, the flakes barely more than fleeting whispers as they drifted across the front lawn.

'I'm sorry about him, he can be a real pain in the arse when he feels like it. Unfortunately that's pretty much all the time.'

'I have no trouble believing that,' Grímur agreed.

Viveca scrolled through the messages on her phone looking for something she was obviously struggling to locate.

'If I had any brains I'd delete these things every now and then but I can never seem to get organised enough. Half of them I've probably never even read. I know I should have showed you some earlier and everything but I didn't really think about it until now.'

'Think about what?'

'Bella sent me a bunch of messages. They were all 'why aren't you picking up your phone' sort of thing, so after a while I just stopped reading them. They're probably just going to bore you but they are from her I suppose. Now she's dead I feel you should see some of them. There were loads though so I'll just show you one or two maybe.'

The garage door opened slowly and Thorgeir's black Mercedes backed out of it and down the driveway. He didn't bother acknowledging either of them as he turned onto the street and accelerated away.

'Straight back to work I see,' Grímur noted.

'Yip, he doesn't spend much time here. He's always working; sometimes he doesn't even bother coming home.'

'He just sleeps at the hospital?'

'That's what he tells Mum. I think he's seeing someone else.'

Grímur had to smile at the way she said it. She really couldn't have cared less.

'What makes you say that?'

'He says he has to work all these nights but I'm sure he's got a place somewhere else where he shacks up with another woman, I can just feel it,' she looked up from her phone and shrugged. 'It's just a feeling I get but I'm pretty sure I'm right.'

'Your mother doesn't suspect anything?'

'I think she does but it's all just part of the deal they have with each other.'

'The deal?'

'Yeah, you know, like when two people are married for the convenience factor. They're both getting what they want out of the deal but one of them might want a little extra and the other one won't say anything because that might fuck up the rest of the deal, the part they like.'

'I see,' he said even though he wasn't entirely sure he did.

'Here's some of them now. Like I said, they pretty much all say the same thing. See what I mean, some of them I haven't even looked at. That's how bored I got with receiving them all. Why she wanted to get hold of me so badly I'll never know. You would have thought that she'd get the message and just give up. Here's one I didn't read.'

Viveca went silent for a second or two and then looked up at Grímur.

'Shit,' she whispered.

'What is it, Viveca?'

She held the phone up so Grímur could read the screen.

> I've done something stupid but I'm not sure what. He's REALLY mad at me but I don't know what I've done. What should I do?

'Who's she talking about?' Grímur asked.

Viveca looked at the screen and shook her head.

'I haven't a clue,' she said.

'And you've never seen this message before?'

Viveca shook her head. She looked as if she was about to cry.

'It's got to be someone you both know, Viveca, please think. How many guys could the two of you possibly know?'

'That's the thing, we don't know any of the same people. We've never had anything to do with each other before the wedding, or since for that matter. The only people both of us would know would be Abelína, and her parents.'

'Kjartan and Helga?'

'That's right.'

#13

THORGEIR WAS RUNNING late yet again. She wasn't going to be happy. Not that she'd been terribly happy about anything much of late, but this was not going to help one little bit. The fickle whims of the fairer sex were still something of a mystery to him even after all these years. So many of life's conundrums had unravelled themselves before his very eyes during his years exploring the human condition, but the female enigma was not one of them.

There were plenty of parking spaces on Barónsstígur so he took one right behind Hallgrímskirkja, in the shadow of the Lord. The white blanket that had covered the city over Christmas was slowly melting away in spite of the light fall that was still coming down. The roads were bare of snow but plenty still remained in the shadowed gardens up and down Leifsgata. He let himself into his building on the corner and jogged up the stairs to the second floor. After a courteous knock on the door he took a second to tidy his hair even though he wanted it to look as if he'd rushed over as fast as he possibly could. Adolfína opened the door and looked at him with something that might best be described as an unamused sneer.

'You're late,' she said as she threw the door wide open and turned her back on him. Thorgeir grinned to himself and closed the door as he stepped inside. Her flat looked impeccable as it always did and he wondered how she managed to be so irritable when she had it so good. Perhaps it was the lack of things to do that got under her skin. He would get a little grumpy himself if he didn't have anything to do with his time and she didn't really have all that much to fill her days with any more. He waited for her to turn and face him but it seemed that she was ignoring him for being late again.

'Unavoidable business, I'm afraid. That irritating policeman was asking questions about Bella.'

'Did her father come to see you?' Adolfína asked.

'Yes, as a matter of fact he did. He arrived at the hospital in the guise of a reporter, asking all sorts of questions about our friend. You were right, he does seem to be letting his emotions run away with him at the moment. If he's not careful I can see him getting completely carried away. Can't you?'

'Speaking of running away, that's what I wanted to talk to you about. Isn't it time we reviewed our plans? I'm getting itchy feet. This time I want you to do something about it rather than just making a whole lot of noise about nothing much in particular.'

'Don't tell me that's what you dragged me here for? I have a full schedule today and I'm already running late. Do we have to do this now?'

As soon as the words were out of his mouth he realised he'd made something of a miscalculation but it wasn't really in his nature to dwell on such things. She turned around slowly and glared at him.

'I didn't mean it like that, it's just I have so much to do already,' he said. 'Can't this wait for another time? We can sit down over dinner one night soon and discuss it rationally. When I have time to discuss it.'

'When you have time to discuss it? How important you make me feel. It's good to know how significant to you I am in the grand scheme of things. I think it's time we talked seriously about leaving. I have a bad feeling and it isn't something we can keep putting off forever. You may think you can but you can't, not really. It's time you made good on your promise to take the two of us away. It's not like I haven't held up my end of the bargain.'

'Adolfína, my love. I am well aware of your feelings regarding our ongoing arrangement here but you've got to understand that I...'

'All I understand, Thorgeir is that you're still with her two and a half years after telling me that it was as good as over. Those were your exact words. I don't understand what's holding you up. Which is it, the musty old wife you can't stand the sight of anymore or that brat of a daughter who spends her life ignoring you?'

'Look, you know you mean more to me than either of them but it's not that easy to just walk away from a life you've spent forty years meticulously constructing.'

Adolfína sized him up with her oh-so-very blue eyes until he could feel himself trying to shrink away from her and disappear into his clothes. He felt like hiding but there was nowhere to turn to in the little flat.

'One day there's going to come that one question you can't find the right answer to. That one finger pointed your way that won't point anywhere else no matter what you say. What are you going to do then? All we have to do is leave now while we're still able.'

'You make it sound all so dramatic. It's not like we're on the verge of wreck and ruin and you're not in a position to be making demands of me,' he said, suddenly finding the anger within him escaping without consideration or consent. 'I don't understand why you can't just be happy with what we've got.'

'Because it's not sustainable. We both knew this wasn't going to last forever and if you're not prepared to call it a day sooner rather than later then you'll ruin everything we've worked to achieve. Tell your wife you want a divorce, pay her what she's due and be done with it or I will make you so very, very sorry. I'm running out of patience, Thorgeir. It can't always be about what you want.'

'You've always over-romanticised this notion of running away together. It may seem like an adventure to you but the reality of the situation is somewhat different.'

'Here we go again,' she flapped her arms in

exasperation and slumped down into one of her armchairs as if resigned already to the upcoming argument.

'You get this flat for nothing, you never want for money. All in all you've got it pretty sweet. Am I wrong?'

'That's right, how could I possibly forget. All I have to do is look after your little tarts downstairs and all is well. Clean up after them and their disgusting clientele, keep the trouble-makers out of the place and make sure the police don't take an interest in any of it. Just as long as nothing interrupts the flow of money into the place you couldn't really give a damn about what goes on here. Far be it for me to want something better for myself.'

'Calm down.'

'All I want is what's best for both of us. What you want is what's best for you and only you.'

'We'll go when the time is right, not because you want to put a premature end to things.'

'It's not premature, that's my whole point. You just don't get it, do you? Any longer and it'll be too late.'

'What are we supposed to do with this place?'

'Put it on the market and get rid of your illegal help downstairs before the police come back to interview them and realise there's something fishy going on here.'

'No one is going to realise anything. Those cops couldn't catch a cold in a rainstorm. We'll move the girls somewhere else for a while and tell the police they've moved on and we've no idea where.'

'What if Gunnar Atli opens his mouth to appease the cops? He knows all about what's going on here and he won't hesitate for a second to tell them if he thinks it will save his skin.'

'What do you mean? He knows nothing of the sort.'

'Yes, he does. I found out he'd been visiting one of the girls downstairs for a little stress relief before he met Bella.'

Adolfína laughed gently and yet wickedly at the same time. She got up and walked across the carpeted living room, put her arms around Thorgeir's shoulders and tucked her forehead into his neck. A long tired sigh escaped her lips before she took a deep breath.

'I'm scared we're going to blow it all just when we should be getting the hell out of here,' she whispered. 'If you can't see that then we're in trouble and we're going to burn.' She lifted her head to look him square in the eyes. 'But before I let that happen I'll tell your wife everything and watch you go up in flames all on your own. You just watch me.'

#14

THORGEIR WAS WORRIED about Gunnar Atli now. As much as he disliked admitting it, Adolfína was right. They had ridden their luck for a long time and it was due to run out sometime. Luck was pretty reliable that way. Next stop was his office at Kleppspítali. The minute he was in he asked for an update on their new patient. Apparently he had slept right through the night without any problems, not surprising considering the sedatives he'd been prescribed, and was now ready to talk. His head wounds would probably still be very tender but he'd been given painkillers and it was time to see just how much of this was an act and how much was real. Thorgeir smiled to himself and told one of the nurses to let Gunnar Atli know his presence was required. They were to let him bathe and see to it that all his dressings were changed. In other words, he was to be made as presentable as possible for the head of the hospital.

Thorgeir made himself comfortable and stretched his legs out over his desk. It would be a while before Gunnar Atli would be ready so there was time to have a think about what he was to do about Adolfína. The situation was slowly but surely becoming untenable. She had outlived her use as far as he was concerned and it was high time he moved on, without her. It wouldn't be easy nor would it be very pretty but it had to be done. He would find someone younger, better behaved and discreet enough to fill the void that would be left by her departure. All he needed was someone reliable to live in the top-floor apartment and keep an eye on the girls below; make sure they didn't get themselves into any trouble and collect the cash off them at the end of every night. There would always be a few trials and tribulations involved in such a business but never anything serious enough to necessitate abandoning the operation.

So far the arrangement had worked very well and if he had to get rid of Petra and Dinka too he was confident he would be able to replace them without too much bother also. Illegal immigrants willing to do that kind of work were as easy to find online as second-hand mattresses. These two had originally come from Bosnia in the back of a truck. They went as far as Ystad in southern Sweden before being transferred to another truck and being driven to Stavanger to service men as they came back from the natural gas rigs. They were willing workers and before too long had earned enough money to pay off their accommodation fees and buy themselves fake Polish passports. After that it had been on to Reykjavik where he'd picked them up himself at the airport and brought them to their present domicile in the city centre.

He'd had it pretty easy with them when he thought about it, he certainly wouldn't get rid of them just for the sake of it. They were both well and truly broken in and even seemed to like what they did. Petra did anyway, it was impossible to tell what the other one was thinking. Either she'd never learned any English or Icelandic or just never let on that she had. For some reason he'd never been able to understand, she preferred to do all her communicating through Petra. But, like most things in this life, they were replaceable. The most important thing was that he not get caught. That part Adolfína had been right about even if her demands to leave the country were way off the mark. He was just about to doze off when an orderly entered his office and informed him that Gunnar Atli was almost ready to see him.

'Which room would you like to use?' the orderly asked.

'Just bring him in here,' Thorgeir replied. 'I'm going to need some privacy for this particular session so my office will be fine. With the amount of time he's already spent here I think we can do away with some of the usual formalities.'

The orderly looked a little puzzled but accepted his orders and left. Thorgeir got himself some coffee and made an effort to tidy the office for a few minutes. It was starting to look a little shambolic but that was only because he never let any of the cleaning staff touch any of his things. He was very particular about that.

A few minutes later Gunnar Atli shuffled into the room looking a little better than he had the day before although his face was still ugly with contusions and swelling. The night's rest had done precious little to repair his battered features and he looked rather sorry for himself. Thorgeir motioned for him to take a seat on the other side of his now clutter-free desk.

'So, how are you feeling today?'

Gunnar Atli just shrugged and tried to rub his face without actually touching any part of it.

'Would I be correct in assuming that you've stopped taking your prescription?'

Gunnar Atli nodded. He felt awful but at least he wasn't in prison. Thorgeir made a show of looking as displeased as he possibly could before continuing.

'You're well aware of the repercussions of such behaviour which makes me wonder why you would do something so irresponsible in the first place. Were you craving attention again or just eager to experiment on yourself?'

Gunnar Atli didn't answer but looked around the room instead, his gaze flitting from one side to the other without actually coming to rest on anything in particular.

'As a result,' Thorgeir continued, 'we've had to put you on several new drugs to calm you down again. All this is setting your recovery back considerably, is that what you want?'

'They think I killed that girl,' he said finally.

'If you look at it from their point of view it doesn't look very good, does it? They also think you pulled that little stunt yesterday to get out of being delivered to Litla Hraun. Once we've got you stabilised they're going to want to take you back there and charge you with murder. You do realise that, don't you? They're not going to settle for any long-term inpatient routine. This time you've gone too far, you won't be able to wiggle your way out of this one.

'Your lawyer has asked me to give you a thorough psychological examination but after that you'll be returned to the tank with all the other little fish. How do you think you'll cope with that, Gunnar Atli? You see, I know as well as you do that the only thing wrong with you is that you're afraid to go to prison and spend time with all those people you don't know and who might not like you very much. This time they're serious about putting you away. Do you fully comprehend what that will mean for you?'

Gunnar Atli fidgeted with one of the butterfly stitches on his forehead. He was beginning to look uncomfortable and nervous and had started to perspire.

'What are you talking about?' Gunnar Atli stopped fidgeting with his wounds and was paying attention now. 'You know I belong here and not in that other place. All you have to do is tell them that and I can stay. If you don't they'll find out about what you've been doing with those foreign girls, and the rest of it. Don't think they won't.'

'Don't you threaten me, you little shit.'

Thorgeir lunged across the table so his face was as close as he could get it to Gunnar Atli's without him actually leaping across the other side.

111

'Who do you think you're talking to?'

Gunnar Atli permitted himself the smallest of smiles to celebrate his victory no matter how small it was. It didn't last for long.

'They're going to find out you were sleeping with her and then they're going to find out you dropped her bags and keys back at the flat and then what? What will they think then? That this nice boy with the broken face was just trying to help out? No, they're not going to think that are they? They're going to think she was trying to run away from you because you become obsessive with girls and when this one wouldn't stick around either, you killed her.'

'You're the one she was trying to run away from, not me. You're the one who scared her so badly she wanted to leave.'

'Who in their right mind is going to take your word over mine? Tell me that. Face it, there's nothing you or your lawyer can do without my help. Either you play the game by my rules or you face the music all on your own.'

Gunnar Atli's eyes were wide and angry now as if he were daring Thorgeir to continue. It was a sneak preview into the Gunnar Atli that lay just behind what he allowed the world to see. Eventually he took a deep breath to calm himself down, leaned back in his chair and smiled.

'You hold all the aces then, Thorgeir. It looks like the next move's yours.'

'I do hold all the cards, don't I? In fact, the way I see it, there's only one way out of this for you now so let me tell you what it is. You're going to want to pay attention to this.'

#15

GUNNAR ATLI WAS so cold he was shaking like a leaf but the chance to spend some time outside the tedious environs of the hospital was just too good to pass up. After being locked away in that tiny observation room for so long, being outdoors again was intoxicating even if it was a very limited sort of freedom. He was accompanied everywhere he went by an oversized giant of an orderly with red hair who wouldn't even tell him what his name was. He had to be new because he hadn't been there when he'd been discharged about a year ago. The guy's only communications were in the form of succinct instructions which he expected to be followed immediately and without question. 'Turn right here,' 'Sit down on the end of the bed and put both hands on your knees,' 'Take this pill, drink all the water and make sure you swallow it,' 'If you make an effort this will go much more smoothly for you,' things of that nature.

He was still trying to absorb everything Thorgeir had told him. Knowing that self-involved sack of wind it was probably nothing more than hot air, just another way to make himself feel more important than he actually was. Thorgeir may have been trying to frighten him with all his talk of prison time and certain doom but Gunnar Atli knew there was at least some truth to what he'd said. His chances at trial, should it come to that, were not good. He hung his head in his hands and gently rubbed the parts of his face that he could bear to touch and scratched at the bits that were becoming itchy as they healed. There were plenty of those. When he closed his eyes he could hear the world around him as if it were a movie playing in a cinema next door. The gentle crunch of someone walking through the snow that had collected around the fir trees and the edges of the lawn, a bird trying to find something to eat while communicating with its mate and the distant banging of chairs being moved across squeaky floors somewhere in the vast building behind him.

The first time he'd entered Klepp he'd been in a similar sort of situation but at the same time completely different. His girlfriend, Nanna, was dead and he'd been seriously injured, his right leg desperately painful and restricting his movement to hobbling around on crutches with all sorts of screws sticking out of his ankle. His inability to find any kind of hope to hang onto had been the primary cause of two suicide attempts. Both times he'd tried to hang himself and both times he'd been cut down just in the nick of time. In the end they had put him in a protected room where he could no longer harm himself. He'd even been on twenty-four hour suicide watch at one point, non-stop surveillance with lights that were never dimmed so they could always keep an eye on him.

It was when his need to self-harm became an obsession as opposed to a habit that he'd been medicated to the point where he could no longer have those sorts of thoughts. The flipside was that he no longer had thoughts of any kind whatsoever, such was the dosage he was prescribed. He became a pharmaceutical zombie, walking the corridors of the facility in a trance-like state, unaware of the time of day or the day of the week. Every day blurred into the next, and then the next and so on.

When they finally cut back on the pills he realised they were pointing him down the road back to the outside world. Dealing with day-to-day society and looking after himself again beckoned and the prospect of having to take charge of his life once more scared him more than being cooped up in a psychiatric ward for the rest of his life. So much so that he fell back into the habit of self-harming again just to let them know he wasn't ready to take that step. Back then all he really wanted to do was hide from the world. And now all he wanted was to stay out of prison. And if he couldn't do that, he would run.

As if right on cue, a chair crashed through a window at the end of the first floor of the hospital building and dropped into the snowy garden below taking shards of glass and bits of broken window frame with it.

Lilja came to the front door and screamed for help at the red-headed behemoth who took a quick look at Gunnar Atli and then ran off to see what was wrong. That was when he knew that this was the moment they had spoken of in Thorgeir's office. He stood up to take stock of his surroundings and to his amazement found he was completely alone. The bare birches rustled quietly down one side of the grounds while the tall well-dressed firs stood guard over the other, but that was it. Not a soul about outside, and inside nothing but the caterwauling of staff falling over each other as they tried to deal with an emergency of some sort that had been predicted with psychic-like ability by the hospital's head doctor.

Gunnar Atli had never been one to look a gift-horse in the mouth. He got to his feet and headed as best he could for the rear of the property. If he could make it through the firs and around the east side of the main building he would be on the road that led to the port before anyone noticed he was gone. There would be one more road to cross and then he would be on his way to Mosfellsbær. Even if they caught up with him it was unlikely he could find himself in any more trouble than he was in already. He could always blame his disappearance on poor supervision and the voices in his head; and at the moment those voices were telling him to get the hell out of there, so that's just what he did.

He limped through the firs and around the side of the main building until the container terminal's perimeter fence stood directly in front of him. In an ideal world he would jump the fence and stow away on a container vessel but with his dodgy leg that was never going to happen. He turned to double-check one last time that he wasn't being followed.

He still hadn't been spotted. Somehow with all the ruckus inside they had forgotten about him and even though that had been the idea all along he was still surprised. Normally, anything that could possibly go wrong for him did and the fact that it hadn't this time concerned him a little. He hobbled as fast as his leg would let him along the fence-line looking for an opening, until he decided that he wasn't going to find one.

When he slowed down to catch his breath he heard a shoe scuff the pavement behind him. He wasn't alone after all and the realisation made him feel sick. What had he got himself into? As he turned to see who his company was he saw a man appear from behind an old shed. The tattooed monolith gave him a look that stopped him dead in his tracks and then lashed out with what appeared to be a chain from a motorcycle. It was long, heavy, covered in black grease and designed to rip a man's face off.

The impact exploded across the side of his face and dropped him to his knees. His lost his vision completely as his one good eye was swamped by a stream of blood. His nose, already in a bad way, felt as if it had been pulled right off the side of his face. A terrifying realisation hit him as he felt himself being dragged by his collar across the footpath and into the back of a waiting car. Thorgeir hadn't arranged the diversion so he could escape, he'd arranged it so he could get caught. He'd been lured into the trap and he'd fallen for it.

Aron Steinn gunned the engine while Kjartan kept a close eye on the injured Gunnar Atli in the back seat. Inside twenty seconds they had disappeared through an unlocked metal gate behind a disused part of the container terminal. The car screeched to a halt, the back door was yanked open and Gunnar Atli was dragged from the vehicle onto the wet concrete. He could feel a gun being pressed against the underside of his chin and hear Aron Steinn's words even if he couldn't see his face. The air was rich with the scents of the ocean.

'Open your mouth without being asked a question and it'll be the last thing you ever do. Give it a try if you want to die, dumbass.'

He tried with limited success to wipe the blood from his eye as he was led along the side of the building. There was the occasional squawk of a seagull overhead but otherwise the place sounded deserted. Everyone was probably still on Christmas leave. Even if he was foolish enough to cry out, there would be no one around for miles to hear him.

'Down there and mind you don't fall in,' Aron Steinn chuckled to himself.

He shoved Gunnar Atli in the direction of a small set of steps that disappeared under one of the piers. There were containers stacked three high down the side of the wharf. Pools of water had collected all around them. Through the blood that kept running into his eye he saw a rat run from the protection of an empty wooden crate under a coiled length of heavy-duty rope. He felt his way down the steps with his feet, desperately trying not to lose his footing and wind up in the harbour. In his present condition he didn't think he'd last very long once he hit the freezing water.

'Stop there or you'll go in, and I won't be fishing you out,' Aron Steinn said.

Kjartan followed the two men down the short flight of steps that took them right to the waterline. There was a small platform at the bottom that must have been used to board small service vessels at some point but clearly hadn't been touched in years. The railings were rusted and slowly falling into the harbour and the steps were worn smooth by the tide and as slippery as ice.

'Now turn around and get on your knees.'

Gunnar Atli did as he was told. He was kneeling with the water lapping over the top of the platform and around his legs.

Kjartan appeared from behind Aron Steinn and folded his arms across his chest. This close to the water the wind was icy and ripped right through his clothes like they weren't even there. Aron Steinn had nothing more than a t-shirt and leather vest on but didn't appear to feel the cold at all.

'Are you Gunnar Atli?' asked Kjartan.

Gunnar Atli nodded and swallowed hard. He could only guess at why they had taken him from the hospital grounds and none of the reasons he came up with were very appealing.

'Do you know who I am?' asked Kjartan.

'No, I've no idea,' Gunnar Atli said through the bloody saliva that had collected in his mouth while he'd been trying to breath.

'My name is Kjartan Jónsson. You knew my daughter. She's dead now, and the rest you should be able to figure out yourself. You're going to answer my questions truthfully or my friend here is going to shoot you and kick you into the harbour where you'll drown like a fucking cat. A kitty cat with a broken nose who can't see very well and won't even know which way it is he's supposed to be swimming with a great big hole in him.'

'Please, you're mistaken.'

'Why did you kill my daughter?'

'What? No, I didn't kill anyone. What's wrong with you?'

'I've already made one deal with the Devil this week and now I'm going to make another one. Do you want to hear what it is?'

Gunnar Atli was shivering all over, he felt as if every ounce of warmth had left his body.

'No. But you're going to tell me anyway,' he said.

'Okay, here's the deal. All I want to know is why you killed my daughter. If you tell me why you did it and admit what you did, then I'll let you live. You'll go to prison, I'll make sure of that, but you'll get to live.'

'No, you've got it all wrong, I'm no killer. Whatever it is you're thinking, you're wrong.'

Kjartan shook his head in disappointment.

'Now you're pissing me off and there's only one way that will end and that's with you getting yourself shot. Think carefully before you speak. And make sure you tell me the truth because if you don't I'll know and you'll find bleeding to death from your stomach a really shitty way to die. That is if you don't drown first.'

'I don't know what you've been told but I didn't kill her. If Thorgeir told you I did he's lying. The guy will tell you anything to get his own way, don't you know that?'

'Is that right? Do you want to know what else he told me? I found it all very interesting so I'm going to repeat it for you. He told me you were in a car accident quite some time ago. That was when you fucked your leg up, wasn't it?'

Gunnar Atli could feel his leg aching terribly with the cold.

'What's that got to do with anything?'

'I'll tell you what. There was someone else in the car, wasn't there? Your girlfriend, the first one you killed.'

'What?'

'That's right, I know all about that too.'

Gunnar Atli threw some water in his face to wash the blood out of his eye and snapped his head up to look at Kjartan properly for the first time. He winced in pain as the seawater stung his eyes and the cuts on his face but still he stared up at him for several seconds before he replied.

'Nanna, you're talking about Nanna.'

'That's right. Nanna was in the car with you and what happened to her? What happened to Nanna?'

'She died.'

'That's right, she died. Now what we really need to talk about is how she died.'

#16

VIVECA WAS SURE she'd heard someone at the front door but when she called out to her mother to go see who it was she discovered the house was deserted. She'd been locked away in her bedroom on the internet for the last couple of hours and hadn't heard Renata leaving. Once upon a time her mother would have let her know she was going out and when she'd be back but those days were long gone.

Grumping to herself she made her way down the stairs to the front door. When she looked out the window there was no one on the doorstep yet she could see a tall thin lady with long dark hair standing on the other side of the street. It was almost as if she was waiting for someone to come to the door because as soon as she saw Viveca at the window she turned and walked off without looking back. Viveca had never seen the woman before in her life but she had definitely been watching the house.

Wondering why she had even bothered coming all the way downstairs she was just about to turn and stomp back up to Facebook when she noticed something lying on the doormat just outside the front door. It was a clear plastic CD case. She opened the door and picked it up for a closer inspection. There were two recordable CDs inside with something hand-written in black pen on them. The writing was very small and hard to read but she was pretty sure what it said. What the dark-haired woman across the street could possibly have to do with a girl who had been murdered the day before she couldn't imagine but there was one way to find out. She bounded back up the stairs to her room, opened the CD tray of her laptop and slid the first disk in.

'Good morning, Ísabella. How are you today?

Goosebumps grew up and down her arms. It was an audio recording of a man speaking in a calm, deep voice; the most menacing voice she had ever heard in her life even though it was a voice she knew. A voice she knew all too well.

'Don't worry too much about the fact that you can't see me because I can't see you either. Well, not your face anyway. You're probably wondering where you are and why you're here but we'll get to that all in good time. You will at least recognise my voice which may give you some sort of clue as to what has gone so terribly wrong for you. Although I would suggest that before you go blaming this bit of bad luck on anyone else that you take a long hard look at yourself. Because, as we all know, you are your own worst enemy.

'You have not been entirely truthful with me. I am afraid that this was a serious miscalculation on your part and the fact of the matter is that you are now strapped by your ankles and wrists to my very special table. You will not enjoy being strapped to this table but that's okay because you're not supposed to enjoy it.'

Viveca shrank back involuntarily from the computer as though it were a snake waiting to strike at her. She couldn't believe what she was hearing. Nor could she understand who the woman was who had dropped the disks off, or why she had done it.

'You cannot see me because your head is covered by a small wooden box that I have designed especially for this purpose. You will be feeling the after-effects of the drugs that have been pumped into you and probably won't feel like talking for a while yet, but you will at some point. When you do, you may feel that screaming will assist you in your efforts to be found or rescued or to escape. It will not. It will only serve to annoy me and that is a bad idea, let me tell you that right now. That sort of behaviour will only get you pain, and lots of it.

'But you may feel like screaming anyway, they normally do. Keeping quiet and compliant is a lesson you will learn one way or another. You can learn it the easy way or you can learn it the hard way but, and you can trust me on this, make no mistake, you will learn it if it's the last thing you ever do and it might just be exactly that.'

Viveca sat down on her bed and put her head in her hands. Was it some sort of sick practical joke? She doubted it very much, in fact she was sure it was real because of the way her skin seemed to be creeping up her arms as if it were trying to disappear under her sleeves.

'You may be wondering how long you are going to be here and what will happen to you while you're here. You are going to be here for a while. How long exactly I haven't the faintest idea but it will be longer than you can imagine right now. So, you may as well get used to it whether you like it or not. You will have to learn to accept what you cannot change.

'As for what is going to happen to you while you are here, we'll get to that in a bit too. For the time being it is probably sufficient for you to understand that it will not be pleasant and you will not enjoy it one little bit. But like I said, that's the whole idea.

'You have listened and learned and used that knowledge to lie, to cheat and to get your own way at the expense of others, namely myself. Well, those days are over. Now you will listen and you will definitely learn a thing or two from me, mainly about discomfort and pain; and you will not get your own way, not today, not ever again. Like I said, better get used to it.'

Viveca flinched when a noise from the front of the house disturbed her trance-like state. She ran to the window to check the driveway but it wasn't someone coming home. It was just the wind blowing broken branches against the top of the house. She took a deep breath to calm herself but could still feel her heart beating so hard she thought it might jump through her chest to escape.

Part of her wanted to turn the computer off and hurl it through the window to the garden below but she knew she had to hear it through to the bitter end.

'The reason why you're unable to speak or think right now is all about two things. The first one is sodium pentothal and the second one is phenobarbital. They are my friends, they will allow me to manipulate the hours you spend conscious and the ones you do not. They are not your friends. You do not have any friends left. You will be administered these drugs as I see fit and they will keep you under my control so that I won't have to kill you straight away. We can have more fun together that way.

'The general outlook for you living a long time now is not very good, let me tell you. The last girl who found herself in that box only lasted a week but that was because she refused to behave. One of them lasted almost a month but she was exceptional in her determination to stay alive. We'll see what you're made of during the next few days. There will be moments of distress for you along with moments of confusion and terror because the drugs will seriously impair your ability to remember what has been happening and this will confuse and upset you a great deal.

'Another reason you cannot speak at the moment is the gag I have put in your mouth. Those things are pretty uncomfortable after a while but it is necessary while you listen to what I have to say. At some point I am going to take it out for a while. How long that is for will depend entirely on you. If you start to scream and yell and shout about what is going on and how you don't like it and all that shit then I will put it straight back in.

'You will need, and I can't impress this upon you enough, to control the emotions and instincts that will tell you to scream for help because it will be a complete waste of time and it will only instigate pain.

'You may not believe me yet about how much that sort of behaviour will hurt you but you will. After the first few times you will be left in no doubt how much pain I am talking about. It will make you wish you were dead until you understand that it will stop if you will just shut the fuck up. That is not to say that all the pain you will experience is avoidable. Far from it. Most of it will be administered just for fun. The pain I am talking about is the pain that will be caused by you opening your mouth when you're not supposed to. Whether that pain exists or not is entirely up to you.

'There are some other rules you need to know about too. You are not to speak unless you are asked a question and then it will be "Yes, sir" or "No, sir" and nothing else. I will not engage you in conversation because you will only waste my time by promising me that you will do absolutely anything for me if I would just let you go. I am not going to let you go but you will take some time to get to grips with this fact, they all do. So in the meanwhile you can save your tears and tantrums for someone else. I am not interested in them and they will only get you gagged and back in the box until you learn that no one cares about your petty little problems any more. You are all alone here and I am the only friend you will have for the rest of your life, however long that may be, so you better get it into your head that keeping me happy is the only thing you need to worry about from here on in.

'Enjoy the rest of your day.'

Viveca wiped a bead of sweat from her brow and waited for the sickness in her gut to pass. It soon became obvious that this wasn't about to happen and she lurched to her feet and ran for the bathroom. She made it to the toilet just in time before she was ill like she had never been before in her life.

#17

GUNNAR ATLI REALLY didn't want to talk about Nanna and couldn't for the life of him think why Bella's father would either. It was in the past, the very distant past. The cold seawater had been lapping over his feet and around his knees until they had all but frozen. His sore leg ached as if it was about to fall off and his face felt as if it already had.

'Tell me what happened to her, Gunnar Atli. Tell me what you did to her,' Kjartan demanded in a quiet but menacing tone.

'I've already told you, she died in the accident. I rolled

the car and she went through the windscreen. Why could you possibly want to know about this?'

'Because I know the truth about how she died. The truth you've only ever told one person before in your miserable little life and now you're going to tell me as well.'

'What?'

Aron Steinn started to grin but in a twisted, menacing way. The more uncomfortable and panicky Gunnar Atli became, the more the muscled giant was enjoying himself.

'What?' Gunnar Atli repeated.

'Say 'what' again and I'll shoot you myself. Now tell me what you told Thorgeir.'

Gunnar Atli looked down at the water lapping all around him and felt something else wash over him. Something dark and frozen that he thought he'd left behind on that snow-covered lava field nine years ago. He could feel it all the way through to his bones as he realised he had been betrayed by the one man he should never have trusted and now his fate lay in the hands of an angry, grieving father and a steroid-injecting lunatic with a gun.

'When the cop arrived he found us injured and lying in the snow. My leg was broken and Nanna was all cut up after going through the windscreen,' he paused to wipe the blood from his face and breathe through his mouth because his nose was no longer available for that particular job. 'I held her hand as she died.'

Kjartan started chuckling to himself. He bent over, grabbed Gunnar Atli by the chin and lifted his head up so he had no choice but to look at him.

'Now tell us what really happened,' Kjartan demanded.

'That is what happened. She died and my leg got all

fucked up,' Gunnar Atli yelled. There were tears welling in his one good eye, once again reducing his vision to next to nothing. Kjartan looked around them to see if they had attracted any unwanted attention yet but the container port and its surrounds were completely deserted. There wasn't a soul to be seen anywhere.

'Lucky it's the holidays, huh? Otherwise someone might hear me do this,' Kjartan said as he took the gun off Aron Steinn, took aim and shot Gunnar Atli in his right thigh. He fell face first onto the platform as he tried to grab hold of his wounded leg. Kjartan signalled to Aron Steinn who moved carefully behind Gunnar Atli and pulled him up onto his knees again. His breathing was coming in short, sharp bursts now and he'd gone very pale. Blood from the wound ran down his thigh and mixed in with the seawater around him. It formed little rivulets that ran across the platform and disappeared over the edge and into the deep beyond.

'Okay, okay, I'll tell you the story. I rolled the car on purpose because she was going to leave me and I didn't want anyone else having her. I thought we'd both die but I was wrong. All I did was fuck up my leg and send her through the windscreen but it didn't kill her. It took me forever to get to her and by the time I did she was almost dead.'

'Almost, but not quite, right?' Kjartan prompted.

'That was when I realised I'd messed up bigtime, she was cut badly and bleeding all over the place so I got hold of the biggest rock I could lift and smashed the side of her head in. I kept hitting her until I could see inside. Then I called the emergency services and pretended to have seen the crash. By the time the cop showed I'd passed out, I didn't even expect him to find us in that storm. I thought I'd die out there too and they'd find us in the morning, frozen side-by-side. It would have been better that way.'

'You've got that right you stupid little fuck because then my daughter would still be alive.'

'I thought she'd been sent to me. You know, like an angel.'

'Well, she hadn't been sent to you and she didn't want anything to do with you either. And when she told you that, you killed her too.'

'No, you've got it all wrong.'

'She had her bags all packed and was ready to leave you behind. You couldn't handle being rejected again so you killed her.'

'She wasn't running away from me, she was running away from him. He drugged her and raped her and was going to make her work for him, sleeping with all those guys to pay his mortgage.'

'You talked her into moving in with you and it probably went okay for a while until she realised what a little creep you really are. That was when she decided to pack her bags and go, and she almost got away too. Admit what you did for once in your life. If you keep on lying to me it's only going to get worse for you. Right now you might not think it can, but believe me, if you keep on lying I will put you through hell.'

'I'm not lying to you. Nanna wanted to leave me for another guy and I did a terrible thing, but it wasn't like that with Bella. She came to me looking for help but she was even more confused than I am. The girl had problems, big problems. She'd pissed Thorgeir off and he was going to kill her. You don't know what he's like, he's a monster.'

'Tell me what you did to her or I'll shoot you again and this time it won't be in the leg.'

'I didn't kill her, you've got to believe me. She stayed with me for three nights, that's it, and then she just disappeared without as much as saying goodbye. She didn't even take her bags or keys with her. I never saw her again, I swear. That's the truth. I didn't kill her and I don't know who did.'

'You fell in love with her because she looked like Nanna. You killed her and then you pretended to go crazy so they wouldn't put you where you really belong.'

'No, I never wanted to hurt her.'

'You figured that since you got away with killing one girl, you'd get away with killing another. They both wanted to be rid of you and you couldn't handle it. Not the first time around and not the second time either.'

'No, I was just trying to help. You've got the two of them confused, can't you see that? I was just trying to help.'

'And how were you trying to help Nanna? She wanted to leave you for another guy so you drove her out into the middle of nowhere and beat her to death with a rock?'

'I was very mixed up. You've no idea what it was like.'

'So you took Bella in out of the goodness of your heart and you tried to help her out and when she didn't want your help you had to stop her from leaving too, right?'

'No, yes, I mean, I wanted her to stay, yes, but I didn't try to stop her leaving. I didn't even know she was going to leave. I don't know how she died, she just did and I was the one who found her and now they want to lock me up for something I didn't do.'

'Isn't that exactly what you deserve? To be locked up where you can't hurt anyone else?'

'No, I don't deserve that. You can't do that.'

'Tell me then, Gunnar Atli. What do you deserve?'

'I don't know.'

'Did Nanna deserve to die?'

'No. No she didn't.'

'What about Bella? Did she get what she deserved?'

'I don't know.'

He pulled a picture of Bella out of his wallet and held it in Gunnar Atli's face.

'Do you even know which one this is? Did you even know who it was you were killing? Did you look at her and see Nanna, is that what happened? Did you look at my daughter and get the two of them mixed up? Because if you did that's okay, all I want is to understand but for that to happen you have to tell me the truth and then I can forgive you. Did you see the wrong girl when you looked at her, is that it? Tell me why you did it and I'll make this go away.'

Gunnar Atli couldn't hold it together anymore, he just wanted out. All these years he'd been tearing himself apart inside because he was the one who should have died in the crash, not Nanna. He'd treated her no better than a dog that had been hit in the street by a driver who didn't want the bother of looking after the mess he'd made.

He should have known it would catch him up one day. Sometimes it took a while, sometimes it took nine years. It was just the way of the world. For everything you took that didn't belong to you, one day someone would take something back. Give and take was what it was all about.

Everybody gave what they thought they could afford, and everybody took what they felt they were owed. Quid pro quo. Sometimes the scales evened up at the end of the day, and sometimes they didn't. Today they were going to stop swinging and come to rest for the very last time for Gunnar Atli.

'I made a mistake,' Gunnar Atli said.

'That's better,' Kjartan replied.

'I got confused. I know what I did was wrong but it was a mistake, nothing more.'

'Admit what you did and I will forgive you.'

'When I met Bella, I couldn't believe it. I thought she'd come back to me.'

'Nanna?'

'Bella came back for me, she wasn't going to leave after all.'

'You mean Nanna? Nanna had come back for you?'

'I made a mistake but she came back to me just like I knew she would. Sometimes when you make a mistake it can still turn out okay if you catch it fast enough. So you see, it doesn't make any difference anymore because the only one I killed in the end was Bella.'

'What did you say?'

'I said, the only one I killed in the end was Bella.'

'That's what I've been waiting to hear you say.'

Kjartan signalled for Aron Steinn to move out of the way and then he fired another round into Gunnar Atli's stomach and watched him double over in agony.

'It's time for us to go our separate ways, Gunnar Atli. The world will be a better place without you.'

Gunnar Atli looked up at him through his one good eye,

his face twisted in pain but flooded with relief. Blood ran through his fingers as he held them over the wound in his stomach. There was shame in his eyes, but there was acceptance too.

'We all learn to live with our mistakes,' he said quietly.

'What?' Kjartan demanded.

'I said, we all learn to live with our mistakes.'

Kjartan put his foot on Gunnar Atli's shoulder and tipped him backwards into the bay. When he hit the water he flung his arms out wide as blood poured from him in every direction. There was simply no fight left in him, like a fish that's finally had enough and is ready to come above the waves. The water washed over his face as he rolled over in the swell and disappeared from sight.

'Well, that's one you don't have to live with any more,' Kjartan said as he stared down into the cold, dark water.

#18

'GOOD EVENING, ÍSABELLA. You seem to be awake again. As you will notice I have been forced to replace the box around your head as well as the gag in your mouth. It would seem that you are not ready for them to be removed. That was my mistake, I apologise. Sometimes I get a little carried away and attempt it ahead of schedule. You were obviously not ready for such freedom as was evident by how upset you became. No matter how many times I explain about the screaming and begging and threat-making they never quite get it into their heads that I am completely serious about the pain that I will inflict when they piss me off. You will now be in no doubt whatsoever as to my sincerity. Your legs in particular bore the brunt of my displeasure and you will find that they will hurt the way they do now for some time to come. I do not make idle threats, Ísabella. Don't try my patience again. If you think that it's impossible for you to be in more pain than you already are, let me assure you that you are very wrong.

'I will have a friend look at your wounds later. If we don't keep them clean they will get infected. Not that I care particularly about the well-being of your legs but the smell will become offensive to me. It appears that you intend to be stubborn and are something of a slow learner so I will have to adapt my methods to your specific traits. I don't think I will be able to take the box off again. Even when you need to relieve yourself I will leave it on. You must learn to behave yourself and I can't think of any other way right now. As for the gag, I don't see that coming out again apart from when you need to be fed and watered. If you don't have something constructive to do with your mouth then all you're going to do is blubber like you did yesterday. I guess it just takes longer for the reality of the predicament to sink in for some than it does for others.

'Since I don't know how much longer you're going to be around, I thought it might be time for us to have this little chat while we still can. My daughter told me the two of you met at a wedding, your sister's to be exact. I informed her that you had told me about your husband and son dying recently and suggested that it would be nice of her if, given the circumstances, she would look after you until you had got yourself settled. At first Viveca just laughed at me. I had no idea why of course. When I asked her to explain what she was laughing at she said it was impossible because you had neither a husband nor a child. She said that you were considered the town tramp wherever it is you come from and that no one would have you, let alone contemplate raising a child with you. Imagine my surprise upon hearing this and how foolish I felt.

'You let me tell you about the anguish I went through over the loss of my son and you sat there and listened with that smug expression on your face. And all the time you were laughing at me behind my back. Didn't you think I would hear the truth sooner or later, or do you just not care about things like that as long as you get what you want? I'm going to take a guess and say that I'm not the first sucker you've tried this shit with, but I can categorically state that I will be the last. Your days of toying with people are over. You probably didn't think that much harm could come from leading people on this way. I wonder if you still think that to be the case or if you've had a change of heart.

'There is no such thing as a small lie, Ísabella. If you tell little ones, you'll tell big ones. People like you like to believe in little white lies because they make you feel better about not telling the truth. You may well think that the only mistake you made was getting found out but you'd be wrong. You let me believe that you knew the pain of losing a child. You accepted my charity and you kept your mouth shut because you were happy to play me as a fool. You took a calculated risk, you rolled the dice, you watched them come to rest, and you lost.

'You have begun your last days on this earth and

although no one can be sure yet just how many they shall number, I am in possession of three simple facts. They will not be many, they will not be pleasant, and you have told the very last of your little white lies.'

As the recording finally came to an end Grímur looked across the table at Viveca. She still looked as pale as she had when she'd walked in off the street with her laptop in her arms like a sick child. There could never have been an easy way for her to learn what her father had become but this had been a particularly distressing way to do it.

'I don't want to ever go back to that house,' she said as she rocked back and forth on her chair. 'Never again, you understand?'

When she'd first walked in she had taken quite some time to calm down but once she had she told him the story of the mysterious dark-haired woman who had dropped the CDs off at the house and he knew it must have been Adolfína. He wasn't sure what the connection between her and Thorgeir was yet but they were obviously in it together somehow. Officers had been sent to her flat to arrest her but they found the place abandoned. Her clothes, money and passport were all gone. Where she had disappeared to was anybody's guess but he suspected she'd already left Keflavík and chances were she was miles away by now. Her bank account with Arion Banki had been closed two days earlier and she'd taken enough cash with her to look after herself for some time. For an unemployed nurse she seemed to have been doing all right.

'No one's going to make you do anything you don't want to. You're safe now, there's no need for you to worry about him any more. He can't hurt you, he can't hurt anyone any more. We'll find somewhere else for you to stay if that's what you want.'

'Thank you, I can't go back to his house. Not even to pick up my things.'

Thorgeir on the other hand hadn't been quite so lucky. He'd received a phone call shortly after Viveca had taken possession of the CDs from someone they now assumed to have been Adolfína. According to eye-witnesses at the hospital he had flown into a furious rage, throwing a chair through his office window into the garden below and then locked himself in. By the time officers arrived to arrest him he had taken a handful of tranquilisers and washed them down with half a bottle of Chivas from his desk drawer. There was no way he could have successfully negotiated the enormous fall from grace that would have accompanied the revelation of what he really was.

He had kidnaped Ísabella Kjartansdóttir and imprisoned her in a dungeon somewhere, torturing and raping her before killing her and dumping her naked body where he knew the blame would fall on Gunnar Atli Davíðsson, and it had so very nearly worked. Grímur was relieved the case would no longer need to go to trial. No one wanted to have to listen to the details of what he had done to her. And from what they had just heard, she had not been the first to suffer such a fate. A search of all his properties would now take place until his secret lair was discovered.

One upside to it all was that they could now release Gunnar Atli, just as soon as they found him. According to Lilja Skaftadóttir he had been sitting at a table in the hospital grounds when the disturbance with the flying office chair had taken place. She'd asked the orderly keeping an eye on him for assistance and by the time they had dealt with that situation he was gone. The poor guy had probably feared that with his track record of psychiatric illness he would never get anyone to believe him. It was unlikely that a man walking the streets in a hospital gown with a bruised and swollen face would go unnoticed for too long though, but so far he had eluded all attempts to locate him.

'How could he have pretended to be my father all this time while he was doing this?'

'He fooled a lot of people, Viveca. It wasn't just you. We've tracked down your mother and she's going to be coming to see you soon. Maybe the two of you can work this out together. It's been a terrible shock for her as well. You're going to need each other's support if you're to get through this in one piece.'

'I don't want anything from her either. I've always felt as though I was imposing on their little club and stepping on their toes. That house was never a home to me because they were never there for me and that's not going to change now. I never meant any more to either one of them than something they could show off to the neighbours. Hey, look at us. We've got a kid too.'

She had always felt that there was something terribly wrong with her family and now she knew what it was. She had spent all these years under the same roof as a monster.

#19

THE NEXT MORNING Grímur pulled up outside a guesthouse on the outskirts of the city centre. The weather had improved slightly; the sky had cleared and the wind had died away even though it was still easily cold enough for more snow. From the shelter of his car he could see Kjartan bringing his bags out onto the pavement. By the way he was moving he looked stiff and tired. It was possible he hadn't been sleeping with all the pressure he'd been under. Grímur lit a cigarette and waited for signs that Kjartan's departure was imminent before heading out into the cold. They caught each other's eye as he hurried across the street. A look of surprise flickered across Kjartan's face and was gone just as quickly as it had appeared.

'Time to head home?' Grímur asked.

Kjartan shrugged and tried to look apathetic which didn't take too much effort.

'They tell me that Bella's body will be released today. She'll be home by this afternoon so I thought I'd better get going. There'll be lots of things Helga and Abelína will need done at home, she's already been on the phone wanting this and that sorted out. You know the way they are.'

'We know who killed your daughter, Kjartan. We've been handed proof of who the killers were and we are in no doubt whatsoever this time.'

'Killers?' Kjartan's eyes didn't light up as Grímur had hoped they might.

'That's right. Thorgeir Alfreðsson and Bella's upstairs neighbour, Adolfína Hallsdóttir. It seems Thorgeir was running a brothel out of the first two floors.'

'You mean, Bella too?'

His response came just a little too quickly. The news didn't seem to be having the effect that Grímur had expected. In fact, it didn't seem to be having any effect on him at all.

'Yes, as far as we know. We've just arrested a couple of girls on the ground floor. They were here illegally, of course. Nice girls, it seems a shame to get rid of them but that's what we'll do. Adolfína's disappeared, she'd left Keflavík before we even knew she was gone. She landed in London yesterday and got a connecting flight from there to

Morocco. Unfortunately, I doubt we will ever see her again.'

'What about Thorgeir?'

'He's dead. Took an overdose after receiving a phone call from our mystery woman, Adolfína. It seems she told him that she'd spilled the beans and he decided it was better to go out on his own terms rather than stick around and face the music. He was dead before we got through his office door. Adolfína dropped off an audio recording at his house for his daughter to find. Then she rang and told him what she'd done before leaving the country for good. That's what you call a cold-hearted woman.

'Thorgeir's daughter listened to the disk and brought it to me. It messed her up pretty good as you can imagine. It's not pretty listening but it leaves us in no doubt whatsoever who was responsible for your daughter's death. We're not sure what Adolfína's role was in it all but there was no way she could have got her hands on this recording without being party to it somehow. She may have even made it without his knowledge. Bella was drugged and kept hidden away somewhere for several days. We're looking for the place as we speak.

'Strange thing happened though. During all the commotion caused by Thorgeir's suicide, Gunnar Atli managed to escape. It's not exactly difficult to get out of Kleppspítali because it's not a prison, but he was supposed to be under constant supervision.

'Hopefully he hasn't got too far though and is still okay. He's not dressed for this sort of weather and he's got nowhere to go that we know of. He's not wanted for any crime anymore so it'd be nice to let him know he's off the hook.'

'There's no doubt it was those two?'

Kjartan seemed unable or unwilling to meet Grímur's gaze as he picked up his bags and put them in the back of the car.

'None whatsoever. Gunnar Atli had nothing to do with it. Just like he said all along.'

'Just in the wrong place at the wrong time?' Kjartan asked as he searched through one of his bags for something.

Whatever it was that he was looking for it seemed to be eluding him. He continued his search as Grímur kept talking to him.

'Seems he never really recovered from that crash he was involved in all those years ago, it really messed his head up. Losing someone close to you that way is just too much for some people to handle. Everyone has a breaking point and I guess he just reached his. You know something else strange? Bella looked a lot like that girlfriend of his who died. Maybe that's why the two of them became friends. They say it works that way sometimes, you'll latch onto someone simply because they remind you of somebody else. Sounds a little crazy, I know, but it's been known to happen.'

'You're right, it does sound crazy.'

Kjartan stopped looking through his bags and closed the car door. He leant against the car and sighed softly. He still wouldn't look at Grímur preferring instead to stare at the ground.

'He never seemed quite right in the head after that but something like that's bound to shake you up a bit. Anyway,

I'm looking forward to apologising to him. He's been through a rough patch but hopefully he'll be able to put it all behind him now. And you, you need to go home and look after your family. You're better off leaving the police work to the police. That's what we're here for.'

'Sure. So you think you'll find him soon?'

'Yeah, he's probably just scared out of his mind somewhere about what's going to happen to him. But as it turns out, nothing's going to happen to him. Isn't that the way?'

Kjartan finally looked up and met Grímur's gaze. Whatever it was that'd had Kjartan preoccupied a matter of seconds ago seemingly gone in an instant.

'I guess so.'

'After everything that guy's been through it would be a real shame if anything were to happen to him now.'

'Sure would.'

'But I'm sure he's fine, just holed up somewhere waiting for everything to blow over. That's what I'd be doing.'

'That's probably what he's doing then. Just like you said, waiting for everything to blow over. I should get going, my wife will be wondering where I am.'

'Of course, that's a good idea. I spoke to her last night actually.'

'Why did you call Helga?'

Kjartan went through his pockets looking for his keys which didn't seem to be anywhere.

'I didn't call her, she called me. She said you hadn't been answering your phone and she was wondering if I knew where you were. Of course I told her I hadn't seen you but she seemed upset, a little bit upset maybe. She said the last time the two of you talked you seemed angry and she was worried you might do something stupid. Her words, not mine. I told her not to worry so much and that I didn't think you were the kind to do anything stupid. You're not are you?'

'What?'

'The kind that would do something stupid?'

'Of course not.'

He finally located his key ring and pulled it from one of his pockets. He seemed relieved to finally have them in his hands.

'That's what I thought.'

'You know how women are, they worry about things too much. It comes naturally to them. Occasionally I've been a bit hot-headed in the past but not anymore. I'm sure we've all done things we're not terribly proud of but you put them behind you and you move on.'

'I guess that's what we do.'

'We all learn to live with our mistakes.'

'What was that?'

'I said, we all learn to live with our mistakes.'

'That's what I thought you said.'

\#

ABOUT THE AUTHOR

Grant Nicol is a happy guy because he lives in Reykjavík now. He loves the cold and the rain and the snow. The colder it gets the happier he gets. If one day he actually freezes to death he'll be really happy.

When he's not enjoying the cold he is also the author of *On a Small Island*. It's set in Reykjavík too and available on Kindle.

#

ABOUT NUMBER THIRTEEN PRESS

PULP

CRIME

NOVELLAS

Number Thirteen Press is building a list of 13 quality crime novellas and short novels, to be published consecutively on the 13th of each month, from November 2014 to November 2015.

For all the latest info and to sign up for the newsletter, or for details about all 13 releases, go to www.numberthirteenpress.com

#

NUMBER THIRTEEN PRESS

WWW.NUMBERTHIRTEENPRESS.COM

#

COMING SOON

Number Thirteen Press #4:

WHEN YOU RUN WITH WOLVES

ROBERT WHITE

13th February, 2015

#

Printed in Great Britain
by Amazon